A FLAWED GOD

Arjun Shekhar is one of the founders of Pravah, a not-for-profit organization that seeks to encourage urban youth to become active citizens. He worked as an HR professional for several years before that, and now runs a consulting firm called Vyaktitva which explores the relationship between an organization and its people. He has used his consulting experiences to write *A Flawed God*, a novel set in the corporate world.

A Flawed God

Arjun Shekhar

hachette
INDIA

First published in 2011 by Hachette India
(Registered name: Hachette Book Publishing India Pvt. Ltd)
An Hachette UK company
www.hachetteindia.com

SRD

ISBN 978-93-5009-057-2

Hachette Book Publishing India Pvt. Ltd
612/614 (6th Floor), Time Tower,
M.G. Road, Sector 28, Gurgaon 122001, India

Typeset in Joanna MT Std 11/13.5
by InoSoft Systems, Noida

Printed and bound in India
by Manipal Technologies Limited, Manipal

To *Ashraf*
for dotting the i's in my spirit
and
to *Saanjh*
for crossing the t

PART I

PART I

Chapter 1

The Clue

Truth, they say, is stranger than fiction. To be honest, I can't recognize one from the other. To me, truth is like fiction's identical twin sister, especially when it's dressed up in words; I wonder if even their parents could really tell them apart.

Take the scene in the window in front of me. A blameless sapphire sky reflected the aquamarine of the Sea of Marmara. A huge gull flew past shrieking its primeval cry and a chilly breeze brought in the smell of the sea.

Of course, the scene was true though the turn of events that had brought me here to Turkey still had me confused. Till a fortnight before, I had been an ordinary corporate executive minding my own business and making a royal mess of it. Now, suddenly, here I was in Turkey at the invitation (typed on a postcard) of a secret guild asking me to join them for a selection meeting for which I had no address.

Alone in an antique land, knowing nobody and with no place to go for tomorrow's meeting, I had taken a quantum leap out of character in coming here.

'I want to go home!' I shouted at the gull perched on a nearby rooftop.

Turning away from the sea, I looked out at the cobbled street from the other window. Far away I could see the domes and spires of the Blue Mosque. It had snowed quite heavily in Istanbul and the streets were still covered when I had arrived early off a red-eye flight from New Delhi. Though by noon, when I got up after a short nap, the last remnants of snow had melted off the cobbled heritage path on which my hotel stood, revealing colourful murals of Turkey's famous eye, under whose vigil no evil could harm you. With all the intrigue I had landed myself in, I could use the eye now. I noticed clay eye pendants festooning the wall of the newspaper kiosk across the street and resolved to pick one up later.

I rummaged in my portfolio for the postcard that had started it all. Instead, my hand found a spare handkerchief tucked away in one of the pockets. I took it out and blew my nose, immediately feeling reassured by the act. I've had a niggling cold ever since I can remember, which became perpetual since my cricketing career imploded and I was forced into this new corporate game.

I dived into the bag again and took out the postcard that had thrown my life into such a tizzy. By now it was soggy and crumpled from use but when it had arrived mysteriously on my desk at noon a fortnight ago, it had been crisp, as if freshly starched. Before email, these postcards had been quite the fashion in India. They were the colour of the yolk of a poached egg. One side was empty and the other had half of it reserved for the address. The one I held in my hand, though, had no address. Just my name – Sanchit Mishra.

I glanced over the tiny typewritten script, my eyes flying over the words, for I knew the contents by heart now.

Hello Sanchit,

I write to you on behalf of the Progress in Work Collective. You may have heard of us. We are a guild of organizational behaviour scientists who run an invisible initiative to put the organization's staff at the centre of its strategy.

We write to you because every year we induct a new crop of core members into our guild through nominations from all over the world. You, Sanchit, have been nominated for the first leg of The Collective's selection process. This is based on your nominator's report on your exceptional one-on-one people-engagement skills, your great teamwork and your contribution in bettering the lot of your workforce. We congratulate you for having made a difference to your constituency and urge you to continue the good work.

For the first phase of your selection process, you are requested to come to Turkey for a daylong event that will commence at 1100 hours (Turkish time) on the 17th of February. Please make arrangements, at your own expense, to be in Istanbul or Ankara by 16th morning. A convenient night coach on the 16th from either of these cities will get you to the location in time for the start of the event on the 17th. You are requested to keep the entire visit confidential, using a tourist visa to enter and leave Turkey.

I turned the card over and read on.

The exact venue will be notified in the English newspaper *Turkish Daily News* where you should look out for the cryptic clue for 6 down of the daily

crossword. Once you have found the
location, please do not make too many
enquiries among the locals.
    The secrecy around the location is of
extreme importance. A group of diehard,
right-wing corporate shareholders have
been trying to disrupt our efforts for
a long time now. And they will stop at
nothing. This caucus seems to take us
more seriously than we ourselves do.
Anyhow, we've realized from experience
that it's better to be cautious. Once
you reach the venue you can let yourself
go; we assure you loads of fun during
the selection process. So tune in,
dance, live. Join The Collective.

There was no name at the end of the postcard;
only a pompous title: Master Craftsman. As peculiar
was the huge holographic seal below the title. In
it a WORK IN PROGRESS signboard stood next to
an open manhole. There was nobody visible, just a
huge spanner and the manhole cover lying beside
the signboard.

Then a funny thing happened. On the signboard,
the words 'Progress' and 'Work' switched places with
each other. Right in front of my eyes! It happened for
a second, and when I cocked my head and looked
again the signboard was back to the original WORK
IN PROGRESS. What was going on? I shut my eyes and

opened them and there it was again: for a fraction of a second the words 'Progress' and 'Work' exchanged places. There was something more. A few heads in silhouette, popped out from the manhole at the very instance when the words switched places. I moved the postcard around looking at it from different angles. The swap happened without warning and without any apparent logic.

I sat down on the bed, all shook up. I must have read the postcard a dozen times but I had missed the switch altogether. What further surprises did that tiny soapbox-sized rectangular sheet of thin cardboard hold?

When I first read the postcard a fortnight ago, though, the dominant feeling I had was of doubt.

'It's a hoax!' I remember whispering to myself, looking suspiciously outside my cubicle to see whether anyone was watching me. I got up and peeped into my neighbour Murgesh's cubicle but he had his long nose buried inside his appraisal form.

Let me explain my initial scepticism about the postcard. It wasn't the secret society bit that I had qualms about; in fact, I was pretty excited about that part for it promised to spice up my boring corporate life. I also loved The Collective's idea of putting people at the centre of organizational strategy.

Might as well stop pretending the organization was a machine where you could set goals, break up the work into little pieces, hand them out to people like prasad while assigning them specific roles and then sit back expecting to reach the destination in the set time.

It just didn't happen that way. Not for me at least. I set goals all right and made plans to achieve them, but nothing went as per plan. I would pause in my journey towards a goal to blow my nose and find that the entire peoplescape had changed. The driver of the vehicle I was travelling in would have gone off for a pee and not come back, and while I went to look for him my boss called telling me I was on the wrong voyage altogether. I would have to start from scratch all over again. Back to the drawing board. I think John Lennon must have had me in mind when he said 'Life is what happens to us when we are busy planning for it.' And that was why the Master Craftsman's glowing description in the postcard of my performance made the entire piece seem like a work of fiction to me.

Far from being the star the postcard claimed I was, I'd struggled in this corporate game. In the last decade, I had already notched three ducks – 'Poor' ratings – in my annual appraisals, all of them in my present company, Frozen Air. In the corporate world, being 'Poor' didn't get you any special privileges like a BPL (Below Poverty Line) card did in real life. Here, you were lucky if our Director General – Godfather, we called him – didn't knock back your stumps and ask you to begin the long walk back to the pavilion.

I had been fortunate to intersperse my ducks with a couple of 'Average' ratings, basically the equivalent of double figures in cricketing parlance; nothing much, just enough to keep my nose above water.

By a curious coincidence, the postcard had landed bang in the middle of the yearly performance appraisal season and, truth be told, it had been a welcome diversion from the trauma of trying to find something worthy to put into my appraisal form.

Immediately I had thought of Pause Daniels. She could surely tell me more about the mysterious Progress in Work Collective and advise me on whether I should take the affair at all seriously. I couldn't ask her directly, of course, due to the secrecy involved, but there were ways to get to the vast store of knowledge in her head. I'd always relied on her for this sort of thing. Some people seem to have a knack for keeping abreast of stuff beyond what is strictly their own business. You know what I mean?

I saw her returning to her cubicle in the distance.

Pause was the Product Strategy Head, a kind of marketing job as far as I knew, but one with a slant on the future that involved planning for the emerging scenarios concerning Frozen Air's extremely sensitive product portfolio. And she'd got this fancy job by being a star performer of the company consistently for the past several years.

Only a week before, I had used my good offices to peek at all her forms from the fifteen years she'd spent at Frozen Air. I'd expected a good record; still, I was shocked to find that her last six ratings had all been 'Outstanding'. It was akin to scoring a double century in each of the last six innings she'd played! Not even God, Sachin Tendulkar, had yet accomplished such a feat.

'Stupid! I am an idiot!' I remember barking at the gleaming white form staring wickedly at me. I needed a coach and who better than Pause to fill the shoes of Guruji, my cricket coach who'd saved me during some dismal dips in form.

'Aiyo, what 'appened da?' Murg's alarmed face had popped up over the cubicle fence. Murg, short for Murgesh, shunned by all of us for being an informer to the dreaded Godfather, never missed the opportunity for a conversation with a colleague. That the colleague usually ignored him was another matter. Being his neighbour, I sometimes took pity on him, and in any case I'd just had an exceptional experience and could afford to be generous.

'Nothing. I should never have left my performance appraisal in my own hands.'

It was a job for Pause Daniels.

'Myee yappraisal in Gawd and Gawdfather hands.'

'Godfather hates my guts. I don't buy my ratings from him like you do by spilling peer secrets.'

'Take it easy, da!'

'You can afford to, I can't.' I got up to find Pause. I walked into the corridor and bent to wet my fingers in the mock fibreglass waterfall just inside his cabin; he'd installed it a couple of days ago, after consulting a Vastu expert who had told him that it would help win him a lot of friends.

I slicked my hair back, watching my reflection in the tiny pool. When I was a teenager my sister had famously described me as 'tall, dark and ahem'. Through school I grew up consoling myself that 'two out of three ain't so bad'. Only later in college did I grow to like my face too; sure my eyes could have been larger and more wide-set, my chin could have been stronger and my cheeks not so gaunt; still, I was better than 'ahem'.

On the other hand, I would put Murg down as quite an 'ahem'. His small chin and beaky nose gave him more than a passing resemblance to a hen; this, and his habit of sneaking around pecking for information was why the name Murg had stuck.

A sly grin broke out on his thin, normally pursed lips. 'What, macchi? Trying to be smart ah? Taking a Pause ah?' His eyebrows went up and down as if they were attached to his hair with rubber bands.

I splashed some water from the pool at him; taking out my kerchief to wipe my fingers, I decided to blow my nose while it was at hand and then walked away.

Sitting on my hotel bed in the Sultanahmet district of Istanbul, I wondered, not for the first time, how the Master Craftsman of the secret guild had got *me* on his radar. Who had nominated me? According to the information I had got off the net, the nominator had to be a core member (limited inner circle who wrote in The Journal) who should have seen the candidate's work from close quarters.

It felt weird to have been under observation for so long without knowing it. Who could have been watching me? Pause had told me of the popularity of The Journal in corporate circles in India and she'd also quoted the grapevine, which whispered of some Indian core members too, but who they were was, of course, a mystery. Their site categorically mentioned that if a nominee was not selected, the nominator stood to lose his own membership. So nomination was a serious business and the stakes were very high. Who had gambled on me?

Well, whoever it was, all I could promise was to try my best not to let them down. I wore my jacket, took my portfolio carefully from the cupboard and slung it on my shoulders. My portfolio, a black leather affair with prominent white stitching on it, had been especially bought from Sadar Bazar in honour of my trip to Turkey.

Stepping out of the lobby, I zipped up my jacket against the wind. I crossed the cobbled street and bought the *Turkish Daily News* and an eye pendant on a chain at the kiosk. Slipping the eye around my neck, I opened the paper. Skimming over the headlines full of the financial crisis that was spreading faster than a nuclear cloud across the planet, I noted that the Turkish stock market seemed to have taken its deepest dive in a decade. It seemed as if every share market around the world was being stalked and dragged down by bears on the prowl. The shareholder caucus, the Collective's arch enemies, wouldn't be in a good mood today.

I quickly opened the daily crossword and read the cryptic clue for 6 down. Six letters – 'The azure part of an evergreen rock'. The answer would give me the secret location of the selection meeting. I didn't have much time to solve the clue; the letter claimed an overnight journey from Istanbul to the location and it was already late afternoon.

I thought of Pause, a crossword enthusiast who would have been able to crack this one for me quite easily. Should I call her? Her father had taken ill, forcing her to go on leave at the same time as me. I wanted to talk to her as soon as I had landed but had refrained, lest it looked too eager on my part. I could call now but she would ask me all sorts of questions. Damn this secrecy. And it wasn't the first time I was cursing it.

The azure part of an evergreen rock. How could a rock be evergreen? Did they mean a mossy rock? And the sea hitting against it was azure? But that would define a million rocks on the southern coast of Turkey. Maybe the evergreen rock referred to the earth (I remembered an American show called 3rd *Rock from the Sun*). And the azure part was the sky. So? Where did that leave me? Hanging between the earth and the sky over the Anatolian plateau!

It was no use. I wasn't any good at all this cryptic stuff. Give me a straight ball at whatever speed and I can hit it for a four, but all this devious reverse swing business had me beaten all ends up.

Throwing secrecy and caution to the wind, I bought a cheap phone card and called Pause from the newspaper booth but her mobile phone was switched off. Now I was in trouble. The wind was straining at the paper, threatening to blow it out of my hands. Clutching it tight, I stared at the clue. It stared back at me relentlessly. Precious minutes later, I was still clueless.

The friendly kiosk owner tried to strike up a conversation. 'I help?'

I looked up, irritated. Did all Turks have a thick moustache and close-set eyes?

'Lost?' he asked, pointing at the open paper I had now spread out on his counter.

He ignored my attempts to ignore him. 'Lost?' He asked again.

'Yes!' I said indignantly.

'How much?'

'What?' I shouted.

'How much lost?'

'Look, pal, either you're lost or you're not. What do you mean by "How much lost?"'

'Bazzar. Share Bazzar.'

'Oh, no, no! I haven't lost anything in the share market. Luckily, I don't have that kind of money.'

'You India?'

I nodded.

'My brother love your country. You lost, he make you win. End of road — his shop. Last but not least. He welcome you special.'

I paid him for the newspaper and walked ahead. Fed large doses of Europeans and Americans, the locals seemed to find Indians an unusual brown treat. Shopkeepers pounced on me like spiders on a vulnerable coloured fly, some to snare me into buying something, others just to play with me.

'Hindu?' a stout man lounging outside his stall asked me.

'Holy cow!' His friend from across the street said with delight written large on his Turkish face.

'Turkish delight!' I muttered, not to be outdone at playing stereotypes.

Both of them burst into laughter. Three shoeshine boys, who'd taken a special fancy to me and had been following me around from the newspaper kiosk, joined in the fun.

Other Turks tried to lure me into their shops. I walked through the lot without stopping – until a hand on my chest got too impolite to ignore. I clutched at my portfolio instinctively. Seeing that the one who'd accosted me was a reedy youth I could afford to take on, I straightened my shoulders, which I had hunched against the cold, and uncoiled my spine to my actual height of 186 centimetres.

'Shah Rukh Khan? You know?'

I sighed and slumped back into my usual question mark. Shah Rukh Khan wasn't a topic worthy of my full potential. I nodded in affirmation, 'Yes boss…' To my surprise, the reedy young man with gelled hair instantly recognized my answer as the name of one of Shah Rukh's big hits.

He grinned, jabbing the air emphatically with his middle finger. He accompanied the obscene gesture with the words, '*Yes Boss*! No. 1.'

I smiled, a bit surprised Shah Rukh had such an ardent fan on the streets of faraway Istanbul. All of a sudden, probably inspired by my smile, the lanky youth with gelled hair broke into a song. I couldn't recognize it because he was mangling the words with his strong Turkish accent though presumably it was from the same film. He urged me to join in; I blew my nose in reply. Other people had gathered around meanwhile and they were all disappointed I wasn't being a sport. The three shoeshine boys hummed along, presumably to encourage me, but I wasn't biting. I had done my bit for this Hindi-Turki bhai bhai dialogue; as far as I was concerned, it was now over. All I wanted was to be left alone to think about the 'evergreen azure rock'.

Thankfully, the song ended after the first stanza as they didn't know the rest of the words, but the lanky Turk hadn't quite finished with me yet. 'Come shop. Take carpet,' he said.

'Not interested!' I shouted, hoping the volume would convey the message in case he didn't understand English. I also waved my hands in front of my nose vehemently to make myself completely clear.

It didn't work. 'Come carpet!' He barked it out like an order this time.

Was he crazy? Did I look like a seth? I had plunged into my meagre savings to make this trip. I had just enough and my calculations certainly didn't include any shopping. 'I can cancel my ticket back to India if you sell me a flying *carpet* for the amount,' I joked.

He didn't get it. He looked at me, dead serious, and said, 'Turkish carpet must.' I looked around at the crowd for support. I was sure they'd agree it was unfair to expect me to buy a carpet as a payoff for listening to a film song I hadn't bothered to buy a tape of back home in India. They didn't! Every single man *and* the three shoeshine boys felt a carpet was certainly in order. A shiver went down my spine. I tightened my grip around the strap of my portfolio.

All I wanted was to decipher the crossword puzzle and I was getting drawn deeper into this unnecessary transaction. How I wish I could have spoken to Pause; she would have unravelled the clue in seconds. Did I tell you she was fantastic at solving cryptic crosswords? It ran in her family.

Pause was always the first person I turned to for help. I recall the day the postcard had landed on my desk. I had immediately gone across to her cubicle for advice.

Floating my long neck over Pause's wall, I had looked at her with the gentle eyes of a giraffe, an expression that would have melted the heart of Milosevic, the Balkan barbarian. Pause, however, was made of sterner stuff.

'Take that mask off, Sancho,' she said, looking up at me briefly and then turning back to her computer screen. 'What do you want?'

'Just thought you might want to pause...' I said, taking a cue from Murg.

'Ha! Guess how many times I have heard that pick-up line?' She raised her eyebrows and trained her fawn-coloured eyes on me.

'Well, blame your dad for it.'

I was sorry as soon as the words were out. Considering I had come to ask for her help, this was hardly the way to start. I blew my nose in remorse. But it wasn't as if I was making anything up. Her father, Jack Daniels, had been an English teacher in a government school twenty miles from Kottayam in Kerala, where they took their literacy (and their liquor) very seriously. She was an only child who arrived almost as an afterthought when her parents were in their forties. Her father called her the 'comma in my life sentence with your mother'. So he nicknamed her Pause, which is the name that stuck with her for life. Hardly anyone called her by her official name: Amla.

That her parents didn't get along was obvious to her right from childhood. They slept in different rooms, ate at different times and engaged with her separately.

By the time she reached adolescence, her mother had contracted a rare liver disorder. Pause bore the brunt of her mother's disgruntlement. This constituted, in the main, of her mother railing at the rank injustice of it all: that while her husband nursed the drinking habit she had had to suffer cirrhosis of the liver. Pause didn't have too many pleasant memories of her mother, who passed away by the time she finished school. After that it was pretty much her relationship with her father that defined her college years. Was it his strong influence that had kept her single till so late in her life? From the devotion she displayed towards her father on the few occasions we'd talked about him, I conjectured this might well have been the case.

Getting Pause to speak about her personal life was like persuading an oyster to give up its pearl. Still, from bits and pieces of Pause's remarks I had put together a collage of Jack Daniels's character. What stood out was his clear preference for introversion. The only company he'd ever sought was that of his bottle. When her mother had died, Jack had pretty much shut himself in. Neighbours and relatives had at first tried to cajole him out but he refused to join any of the ceremonies or get-togethers. Slowly, everybody began to shun the Daniels household. As a result of the exclusion, Pause and Jack were forced to spend all their evenings at home together. In the early years, they mostly read in different rooms. Even dinner was eaten separately. Later they found a common interest – the cryptic crossword. Even now her octogenarian father wrote his infrequent postcards to her in the form of crosswords.

Pause's other passion was theatre. She had directed and acted in many Malayali plays as a graduate in Trivandrum, which she claimed had changed her attitude to life. From a lonely, cloistered existence as a teenager she was suddenly catapulted into limelight on the stage and into a whole new world of friends and experiences – learning opportunities, as she called them – which left her more optimistic, confident and worldly-wise.

She used her theatre skills to good effect to put me in my place now. Her wide mouth turned down and the back of her right fist touched her forehead as she delivered a sharp repartee to my thrust about her father's punctuation fixation. 'Just my luck! I wait all day for a knight in shining armour to sweep me away on his horse but look who gallops by on his donkey – Sancho Panza!'

When she first began to call me Sancho, not long ago, I had mistakenly assumed it to be an affectionately shortened version of my name, Sanchit. Till I found out that she had christened my immediate boss, the Human Resources Director, Don – as in Don Quixote, Cervantes's notorious knight of La Mancha. She said the HR Director's passion for courting trouble over gallant but foolish interventions matched, even surpassed, the Don's penchant for getting himself into a mess over his Good Samaritan causes. She explained that Sancho Panza was Don Quixote's valet, who'd saved his master from many a mishap. Don picked fights against worthier opponents and Sancho Panza picked him up afterwards.

I had protested, of course. Not because of her allusions to the numerous occasions I had been the fall guy for a misadventure initiated by my boss. What I found difficult to accept was the donkey she said Sancho Panza was partial to. In India, donkeys were ridden by only madmen or fools, or those in disgrace. There are still reports of people from such and such village blackening a criminal's face and making him ride a donkey through the streets. But by the time I had figured all this out, the name had already stuck. Though, thankfully, not everybody knew about Sancho Panza's preferred vehicle or at least they didn't remind me about it every once in a while like Pause did.

I swallowed her insult, realizing any further sparring would only harm my chances of being accepted as Sachin Tendulkar's pupil. I said humbly, 'Touché! You know I'm unarmed in a battle of wits against you, Pause. I was just looking for shade to sit in and swap stories.'

'I accept your unconditional surrender. I hope you have an interesting story to tell me because you are dragging me away from something really important.'

'Well, to me it's a matter of life and death! You can decide whether you find it interesting or not... over tea and pakoras? You do need a break.'

'Still an hour and a half for lunch. Pakoras sound good.' She rummaged around for her wallet inside her cavernous black bag. Meanwhile, my eyes fell on her appraisal form lying smugly closed in one corner of her empty table. It reminded me of a famous motorcycle ad tag line. 'Fill it, shut it, forget it,' I said aloud.

'What?'

'Nothing.' Taking a quick look at her screen, which had gone into screensaver mode by now, I asked, 'What are you doing that's so important?' I didn't really expect her to tell me. If it was difficult to get Pause to talk about her personal life, it was impossible to get anything about her work out of her.

'Oh, routine stuff,' she said as always. She was being modest, for her work was far from routine, evinced by her frequent call-ups to Godfather's office even though she reported to the Marketing Director; she was secretive to a fault about whatever she did with him. 'Someday I hope to break through your routine answer.'

'Come, come, let's go to the cafeteria,' she said, signalling that the topic was closed.

Our office, occupying the entire floor of one of the oldest high-rises in Connaught Place, had an open-plan design. Two main arteries gave the confused maze a semblance of order. Between them they enclosed two lines of cubicles. The corridor on the far side was what we called Janpath (path for the common man) because across it sat the staff and assistants. Janpath ended deep inside the bowels of the office past a cafeteria into a small room that passed for a library. Pause's cubicle let out on the other artery, Rajpath (path for the rulers), because across it were

five well-appointed rooms that housed the Directors
and their secretaries. Between the two arteries sat the
entire middle and senior management.

At the start of Rajpath, in the main lobby, was
a display case housing a handful of refrigerant gas
cylinders. From this clutch of cylinders emanated
a powerful tangy, lemon-drop smell, which stalked
every corner of the office as if a big cat had marked
its territory. There was no mistaking who the big cat
was: it was Godfather who more or less ran all the
departments, and the other four Directors were as
ceremonial as those cylinders in the display case. But
we continued to show them deference, pretending
we didn't know they had been caged.

I nodded respectfully to the Finance Director who
had passed by just then.

As we cut across to Janpath, I remember
contemplating whether I should use my clandestine
knowledge of her ratings to begin our conversation
appreciatively. I had to be careful because it could go
either way. She wasn't averse to flattery but it didn't
sit easy with her either. I decided to go with praise.
Being partial to romance novels, in particular Bills
and Moon, I had noted the consensus among all their
heroes on praise being a 'woman's stiletto'. (The
difference between the phrases 'Achilles' heel' and
'woman's stiletto' is that while the former refers to a
chink that can be used to defeat your opponent, the

latter is a path to winning them over. Subtle difference, but worth pointing out to a discerning audience.)

As soon as we took one of the moulded plastic tables at the far end of the cafeteria, the boy supplied us with pakoras and tea without us needing to order any. I was nervous about bringing up the topic of appraisals; they were considered to be too intimate to discuss even between close friends. I wasn't hungry but I bit into a pakora to disguise my apprehension.

'You should have washed your hands, Sancho!'

Ignoring her, I said through a searing mouthful, 'Pause, I awnted to ongatulate you... I just 'earnt oo've bin rated ow'standing continuously f' fix years.' I splayed my oily fingers for emphasis.

All of a sudden she blushed and on her dusky skin the effect was marvellous. I can't name the colour that her cheeks took on but there was a hint of a sunset, a dollop of chocolate, a goblet of claret and, yes, there was that glow in her large fawn eyes that suddenly made the dim cafeteria look as cheerful as a night sky lit up by a million fireworks.

This was by far the best reaction I had ever elicited from her. I resolved to write to Messrs Bills and Moon telling them how much on the nub their authors were about starting a conversation with praise. Before I could say anything further, she spoke with a coyness I would never have imagined existed in her no-nonsense character. 'Thanks,' she said. 'You're quite a sneak, though. How did you find out?'

'Oh, I'm good at this sort of thing.'

'At being a sneak? Hmmm… You're pretty good at a lot of other things too.'

'Name one.'

'Well… let's see… ah, here's one – saving your boss from ruin.'

'Hardly something I will be rated highly for.'

'Rating? Where are you going with this, Sancho? Why is the appraisal such a big deal for everybody in this company?'

It wasn't. In fact, appraisals were part and parcel of the human condition! Didn't we start evaluating from the moment we got up from our beds? 'The toothpaste is too salty'; 'why was she being so bitchy last night'; 'my mind is slow today'; 'the boss looks like he's had a fight at home.' And weren't we judged by others since we were born, either formally – by my doctor, my school teachers, my cricket coach and selectors, my bosses at work; or informally – by my parents, my friends, my team-mates, my peers? Our race was fixated with measurement. I had been sized, sliced, diced, julienned and cut open in a myriad ways. So appraisals were hardly my problem. What was frustrating for me was that I hadn't got used to doing it to myself. What I was obsessing about was the self-appraisal I would have to write in my appraisal form for my discussion with my boss tomorrow.

I gulped down half the cup of scalding tea at one go. Pause had a hint of alarm in her eyes.

I fingered my throat and cleared it dramatically, 'Ahem! I am used to being appraised by others. That's not the problem; it's this *self*-appraisal I can't handle. What do I write in my form? Should I be honest? In that case, I will be judged harshly. And I do so want to rise above my mediocrity, Pause.'

'Above mediocrity is only anxiety, Sancho...'

'How can you say that? Not after your record. I was just writing up the form for my review discussion tomorrow with Don and... ahem... and I was actually wondering how... you know...' I trailed off hoping she would understand.

'Ah, so that's it! You want me to help you jazz up your form so you can get your first Outstanding rating in Frozen Air, right, Sancho?'

Outstanding? Was she kidding? I would have been ecstatic with a 'Good'.

'Actually...'

'What's the problem? No bright spots in the year?'

Did I discern a chuckle in her voice? 'First rule of therapy – the therapist never laughs,' I said sternly.

'Therapist?'

'Well, you are my *performance therapist* now!'

Suddenly she became dead serious and said, 'Okay, I accept your case.' That's just how she was.

'Now, Sancho, the most important thing to remember is that though your first-level discussion tomorrow may be with your immediate boss, the real audience for your autobiography is Godfather, who we all know decides the final rating. The second, even more important thing to note is it doesn't matter what you *do*, it only matters what you *say* you have done and what you say you are *going* to do. A story presents what's not present.' I told you she was smart. 'And, Sancho, your story needs some special effects. Like in those fantasy films.'

'I don't know of any special effects that can light up darkness.'

'What's all this depressing talk about darkness? We have to think positive...'

'Easy for you to say! You are going for your seventh outstanding rating like Lance Armstrong in the Tour de France. I am the unknown blue jersey among the last ten, pedalling away furiously to finish within the stipulated time.'

'Didn't Armstrong have cancer or something?'

'Yup, he had testicular cancer and when they cut his balls off he actually came back and gave the performance of a lifetime to win the Tour de France for the sixth time.'

'Hmmm... I always thought too much was made out of this balls thing. You know, the macho bit. Getting that out of your head helps you think better. First things first, let's get your testicles out of the way.'

'What?'

'Change your outlook, I mean. Make you think more like a woman.'

I blew my nose to disguise my bafflement. 'How do you mean think more like a woman?'

'For starters, you wouldn't take yourself so seriously. You don't need to go around looking for others' good chits to know you are outstanding, Sancho.'

The cuticles in my toes became agitated by the unexpected praise. The compliment took nanoseconds to reach there from my head and they began to tingle. But wait a minute. Wasn't it a backhanded one? She made me sound desperate.

'That's easy for you to say. You've got six of those good chits already. It's always the guys who have the money who say it's not worth it. The fancy MBAs will always denounce their institutes as "time-pass". If you have the pedigree, you can turn up your nose at it. I suppose that's the way to climb to the next level. By rejecting the one you are on.'

'You'll see that it's not all it's cracked up to be. Anyway, why don't you come home after work? We can talk more.'

'But... there's hardly any time...' I protested.

'Tch! You are meeting Don only tomorrow. C'mon! We'll leave together at... around eight? Toodledoo... oh yes, can you please pay for my chai?'

I clucked my tongue in irritation. She got up and tousled my hair like I was her pet poodle or something. Now this was too much. She was taking me for granted. On the spur of the moment, I decided to spring my nomination to the Progress in Work Collective on her. Before the door could bang shut behind her, I sprinted across the cafeteria and deftly jammed my foot in.

She turned around at the noise of my shuffling feet. 'You are a fast mover,' she said in the 'pet poodle tone.'

'By the way, you know the Progress in Work Collective?'

I was pleased to note my question startled her out of her smugness. She looked at me quizzically, her nose twitching, as if sniffing at my sudden interest in The Collective to check for anything suspicious behind it. She nodded tentatively. 'Of course, everybody knows about them.'

'I don't think I do.'

'I'm surprised you don't, especially since you're from Human Resources.'

'I am not from Human Resources,' I wanted to tell her, but didn't. After my cricketing career had combusted, I'd got a break as a medical representative. When I realized I was way behind the competition due to my late start in the corporate world, I had bought myself a degree. Where was the time to study for it? Without it I felt I would remain the perennial twelfth man. It happened to be in HR because it was the only one I could afford. The degree had got me an executive position in Frozen Air, though considering my poor form it didn't ensure that I could hang on to it.

'Why should an HR guy know this Collective?' I played safe.

'Because The Collective claims they're going to save "work" from the four-letter curse it's become. Aren't you guys in HR supposed to do that too?'

'Curse?'

'Do you enjoy coming to work every day?'

'Hell no!'

'Then go to their website,' she said calmly. 'And if you prefer something more physical, our library stacks the entire set of their quarterly journals. Also a site called Human Chain tracks The Collective extensively. We can talk more about them in the evening when we meet. But tell me, Sancho, aren't they way out of *your* league?' She searched my face for a reaction. 'You are desperate for an "Outstanding" rating, while they work anonymously, wanting no certificates. Work itself gives them meaning!' Then she was out of the door.

The taunt unsettled me completely; I hadn't expected her to take undue liberties just because I was needy. 'You'll pay for this...' I shouted to no one in particular.

'Oh no, she won't, no credit here,' the cafeteria owner said in a warning tone. 'I've told you that before...' I shook my head, picked up the bill he'd slid across the counter and took out my wallet to pay. Suddenly, Pause popped her head back in and said,

'Oh, by the way, I'm also going to call Lokesh home tonight.'

Fraud!' I exclaimed. Since Pause hadn't stayed to see my reaction to her announcement, my eyes went back to the bill in my hands.

The cafeteria owner drew himself up behind his counter, a frown on his face. 'Just because I raise the price of a plate of pakoras by 50 paise, you call me a fraud? I won't have any of this here. Do you know how much the potato has climbed in the past fortnight?'

I paid up quietly; I was in no mood for any discussion with him on potato prices. My mind was on how that other potato, Lokesh's stock had been rising steadily with Pause.

Ever since Mcsinki, the strategy consultants, had come into our company, both of them were forever closeted together in secret discussions with Godfather and the consultants. As the Planning Manager for Frozen Air, Lokesh had unbridled access to Godfather, and was one of those few masochists who enjoyed entering Godfather's 'zone' of their own volition.

I, on the other hand, believed that in a fight for survival, one should never lead with one's chin. When my own business was in the doldrums, who was I to go around poking my nose (or chin for that matter) into the company's business affairs? Though, when I caught snatches of these lofty conversations between Pause and Lokesh during lunch, which the three of us always ate together, I would pretend to be interested. Of late, they had become very careful about choosing what they spoke about in my presence and if one of them strayed into forbidden territory the other would gesture by zipping their lips. The intrigue had become almost unbearable. More infuriating than to be shut out like this was their ganging up against me.

It wasn't strictly my business as to what Lokesh and Pause had going on between them and what part of it was official and what was not. Still, for her to invite him to our therapy session was sacrilegious. Didn't she know that in therapy three was a crowd? It was like the tepid promise of friendship versus the intensity of love, the scatter of a triangle against the precision of a straight line.

It didn't help that Lokesh had never trod a straight line. He loved to ramble like a directionless bumblebee. Which was the reason that his nickname was longer than his given one – Loquacious some of us called him. He was the kind of traveller who professes the journey to be as important as the destination. I, on the other hand, was trained to run fast between the wickets. Getting to the other end before the ball shattered the stumps was of paramount importance. Nobody was interested in how many steps you took or how elegant you looked while getting there.

I walked back to my cubicle, mulling over Pause's parting shot about The Collective being out of my league. Was it her way of pushing me beyond my comfort zone? Guruji, my cricket coach, had used the same taunt when I had expressed my desire to play for the Indian cricket team. Unfortunately, his gibe had come true, when, on the brink of making it to Team India, I had self-aborted my career by getting entangled in that match-fixing scandal.

Another chance of making it to the highest level beckoned. If Pause was to be believed, I was once again on the verge of breaking through into a very select squad. The selectors had invited me for trials in faraway Turkey; obviously they were interested and felt I had the talent. It would probably come down, again, to my tendency to self-destruct. Would I be able to overcome this fatal flaw?

I reached out to the false waterfall in Murg's cubicle and absent-mindedly ran my fingers through the water. I took a deep breath and looked at my reflection in the glass wall across the corridor.

'Get real, Sancho. Is it a dream you're chasing?' I asked my reflection, flicking water into my eyes. 'Or your own tail?'

'Woof, woof. Bow wow,' said Murg.

'Same to you, Kukdoo Koon. Cluck cluck.'

Standing on the cobbled streets of Sultanahmet, surrounded by a sizeable crowd now, I took out my phone to call Pause for cryptic crossword therapy. If she could tell me what the clue meant, I would be able to face up more confidently to the reedy youth who wanted me to buy a carpet.

Alas, her phone was still switched off.

To avoid a public confrontation I walked into the lanky young man's shop (it was the last but not least, at the end of the street) where his elder brother, a substantial man with a typically thick Turkish moustache, took over from him. The young angler had hooked me, now it was his turn to watch (and learn) from the sidelines how the master would reel me in. I took in the small, overheated, overcrowded shop smelling of damp wool. I realized I was now quite tense about how I could escape the Turk duo's clutches. 'If your opponent knows you're afraid, he'll get your wicket in that over,' Guruji's warning rang in my ears. I found my kerchief in my hands though I didn't remember taking it out, and blew my nose absent-mindedly.

A small crowd still lingered outside the shop. I distinctly remember seeing the shoeshine boys following the story through the glass door.

'Hello, friend! From India?' His English was much better than his brother's at the newspaper kiosk.

'Yes,' I replied carefully.

'What part?'

'I live in Delhi.'

'Beautiful place.'

I had never heard it being described that way to me and would never have described it so to others. But we Indians were known to be patriotic, more so abroad. So I agreed reluctantly with the Turk, 'Quite beautiful. Have you been there?'

'Many times.' I was surprised by his answer (later I found out hundreds of Turks travelled routinely to India). 'I love Karol Bagh.' It was a district in central Delhi famous for its overcrowded bazaars, offering huge bargains in anything, from women to carpets, and attracting tourists across the budget spectrum.

Carpets! Ah! So that's where he gets them. A sigh of relief escaped my taut body. 'Your carpets are from India!' I blurted out almost accusingly.

'Mainly Kashmiri,' he admitted sheepishly. 'We have beautiful kilims from there as well.' With a broad sweep of his arm he motioned to a wall on my right.

I looked politely at the kilims as I sipped Turkish tea from an ornate glass tumbler, which had appeared magically in my hand. I recognized a pattern that was on a kilim my grandmother had bought years ago in Kashmir, which still adorned my mother's home. I wondered if carpets still lasted through many generations as they did in those days when producers were not yet savvy about the tricks of obsolescence and upgrades.

'No carpets?' With his keen sales instinct, the shop-owner realized he'd travelled as far as he could on the carpet line. 'Take jewellery then,' he changed tack, 'I only keep the most special lapis lazuli from Afghanistan.'

Didn't he sell anything Turkish at all? I'm sure if I had probed deeper he might have turned out to be a foreigner, maybe a Kurd or an Armenian.

'You won't find the azure rock in India,' he continued, trying to hustle me into taking an interest in his wares.

His last words achieved much more than he'd hoped. I jumped at him in excitement. 'AZURE!! Did you say azure?'

He drew back sputtering, 'What? What?'

'Mister, you just solved a mystery. Lazuli means azure, is that right?'

'Yes. And lapis is Latin for stone.'

'And this lapis lazuli – was it a rock popular in ancient times as well?'

'Yes, since the time of the Egyptian Pharaohs.'

'Evergreen... hmm...' I wondered aloud.

'No, no, only blue.' He was looking confused now; I was proving to be a difficult fish to reel in.

I stared at the blue network of veins on my forearms. 'Do you have a map?'

Again, he recovered fast. 'Yes, you want to go south? My brother runs tourist agency.' How many brothers were they?

'Yes, I might use his services, but first a map.'

I slung my portfolio hurriedly across the back of a chair and opened the map with eager hands. 'Where you want to go?' He enquired. I could have asked him about Lazuli but in deference to The Collective's advice to keep it all under wraps I decided to look for it myself. It took time because I was convinced it was on the southern coast; finally I found it in the middle of the plateau. There it was! Lazuli, near the Ihlara vadisi in South Cappadocia. The puzzle was solved and I felt proud at having done it myself, without Pause's help. It felt like the world was perfect, a prayer had been answered, and the round peg after flirting with squares and triangles was now neatly slotted into its rightful place. No wonder these crossword enthusiasts went about with that smug look on their faces. This was deeper than meditation, more sublime than sport, and a faster high than any drug.

I thanked the shopkeeper for all his help and took his leave. 'But... what about tour to south...'

'I've changed my mind!' I turned to walk out. I thought I might have broken his heart but he was too hardnosed for all that. His only interest was in not letting his supper escape. 'Want belly dancing, better than Indian cabaret?' I hung my head down and gave him a resigned smile. I felt a tiny bit of guilt, for to be fair to him the poor chap had tried a range of baits.

At the door the reedy youth came alive, 'Turkish bath?'

As I strode back onto the street with a purposeful
shake of my head, I marvelled at their tenacity. Man,
could they hustle in this country!

'Namaste to Shah Rukh Khan,' was the parting
shout I caught as I crossed the street.

CHAPTER 2

The Ride

The coach to Cappadocia was well-appointed, even boasting a cramped but clean toilet. The massive bay windows were securely sealed against the bitterly cold night air. The balmy temperature and my lack of sleep the night before lulled me into a snooze.

Not for long, though. I heard a bark somewhere in the upper reaches of my consciousness; unfortunately it seemed near enough for me to have to have a look. I forced myself out of the well of sleep and found a massive shaved head peeping at me. I dragged myself out to meet the tough-looking liveried attendant who reminded me of a retired WWF wrestler. He was saying something seemingly very important in Turkish.

'I don't understand. You speak English?' I said after his third attempt. I would have been more than happy to comply quickly with whatever he wanted me to do and get back to my nap but I couldn't get the drift of what he wanted.

The wrestler pointed at my socked feet with a vehemence reminiscent of a sanitation inspector who'd found a cockroach in the soup. I craned my neck beyond the portfolio on my lap to get a better view of my miscreant feet. A bit earlier I had taken off my shoes in readiness for a spot of sleep; there was a thumb-sized hole on the toe of my right sock but that was hardly something he could pull me up for. I glanced helplessly at my co-passenger (a portly old woman in traditional Turkish dress); her eyes were shut and she was mumbling something to herself as she fingered her rosary. I evinced the same uninvolved attitude in the other passengers in the immediate vicinity.

The wrestler went away, a little exasperated at not being able to get through to me. Hopefully he would come back with somebody who spoke English.

I couldn't go back to sleep knowing he would be back. My mind turned to Lazuli. Was it going to be the turning point of my life? Would I be plucked from obscurity to be part of a team of superheroes? Or was I making too much of it? Whatever transpired in Lazuli, one thing was for sure, it was going to be a momentous journey – that I could tell in my bones... but only if the wrestler would leave them intact.

He was back! Alone. Though his tone hadn't been too unfriendly to start with, on this, his fifth attempt, frustration was creeping into his body language. Telltale signs – little beads of sweat on his face, bulging veins in his pig's neck and an increasing edge to his voice – didn't augur too well for my passage to Cappadocia.

I looked down at my feet. Maybe taking my shoes off was the infringement he was blowing the whistle for. I knew the Turks were finicky about smell in their public transport. I recalled the attendant generously splashing jasmine itr on our hands as we'd got on. I hurriedly wore my shoes and then looked up hopefully at him.

No luck. He drenched me in choice abuse – the standard way to communicate with a rival wrestler in a WWF match. It did raise my hackles a bit but my lanky frame was no match for his rippling muscles, so I lowered my hackles. The way his bulging neck had ballooned, it looked like a toad's throat, and if he got any angrier his bow tie would certainly pop. The clutch of locals around me had started to get interested in my predicament now and the one with coloured hair across the aisle was sniggering openly. The famed Turkish hospitality obviously hadn't boarded this coach. Was it just a façade for the street hustlers in Istanbul?

I looked out into the dark night, contemplating my misdemeanour once again as the whole bus waited for me to act. Since a response, probably my last chance, seemed to be in order, I took out my kerchief and blew my nose. The wrestler, far from satisfied, snatched the kerchief from me and tore it to shreds. At this breathtaking display, even the portly old lady next to me was forced to interrupt her mumbling. She goggled approvingly at this unexpected entertainment.

After his energetic outburst, suddenly, the wrestler grew calm, as if it was all over. That really scared me. My hands began to tremble, beating an inaudible tattoo on the portfolio in my lap. My feet were sweating and I could feel a hot flush spreading from my groin towards my chest. I readied myself for the inevitable roughing up but luckily (or so I thought then) a voice from up front distracted the wrestler.

'The attendant wants your bag. Give it to him, you deaf dodo!' It was a man's voice speaking perfect English. There was something sinister about the way he'd barked the order, like a man used to being in command. He had the rasping voice of a lifetime smoker. From his accent you couldn't place his nationality. In fact, it was hardly an accent at all, quite neutral, something every agent in the call centre industry in corporate India aspired to. Global English, I believe it is called.

The wrestler, who obviously loved a fight, found the intervention pregnant with the possibility of expanding his quarrel. After disappointing old me, the spunk in this new adversary was clearly more promising. He let loose an intimidating volley of

Turkish phrases towards the man. But the smoker gruffly told the wrestler something in Turkish that seemed to shatter the latter's hopes of a battle. He shut up and glowered at me menacingly, waiting for me to give up my portfolio.

I raised my head meekly, trying to locate the owner of the raspy voice. 'This is hand baggage. I'm not giving it to anybody,' I said in my gruffest voice to the front of the bus as I defiantly clutched my portfolio.

'What's that? Stop squeaking. Speak up like a man.' The raspy voice floated back to me.

I wasn't about to let the Turks intimidate me into handing over my portfolio. I repeated myself with a little more spunk in my voice.

'It's a rule in this coach,' said the Turk with the raspy voice. 'He's only going to put it away for safekeeping in the cabinet in front, like all the others, you ignorant idiot. Give it to him now before he gets too enraged for me to hold him back.' The whole act looked a little suspicious. What did they know about me? And did they think I was carrying the papers in my portfolio? That had to be it. How else could one explain the insistence? I clenched and unclenched my fist.

'No. I have a right…'

The wrestler lunged for my lap and would have uprooted my family jewels if he hadn't connected with my portfolio first. I hung on to the strap but not too tenaciously, knowing it would be impossible to hold it against the inevitable jerk from the wrestler. So when the pull came, the wrestler fell backwards onto the youth with coloured hair who, I couldn't help noticing, stopped grinning pronto.

Recovering his feet, the wrestler carried my portfolio gingerly in his extended arms like it was a gift for a king. I craned my neck and saw him handing it over to the Turk up front, rather than depositing it, as professed, in any cabinet. I stood up to identify the rat I had smelt earlier but I could only see the back of his head. The seated Turk took his own time with my portfolio, rummaging through all the papers. There was no doubt about it now. There was conspiracy afoot! They must have been alerted about my having the folder with the deadly ideas on my person; the folder I had begun to call The Quiver because it contained in its spine a score of double-sided pages, each as lethal as a poison arrow, each capable of fatally wounding the Corporate underbelly. Which could mean only one thing – the guy up front was a dreaded Keeper of The Shareholders' Conscience, arch enemies of The Collective. There had been an oblique mention of an enemy group, a shareholder caucus, in the postcard, though it was only later on the day I received the postcard, when I was surfing the net in the library, that I found an article devoted to the war between the two groups.

It wasn't good form to be surfing the net for anything beyond your work; everybody had free access but Godfather's spies (most of us suspected Murgesh was the leader of the spy ring) had formulated ways of tracing the sites you visited and reporting transgressors to Godfather himself.

Suddenly, I remembered the machine in the library. I would have to be careful not to be seen going in, though. I picked up some random papers, assumed a worried expression on my face and walked fast down Janpath. Normally, when I had nothing to do (or didn't feel like doing what I had to do), I walked the corridors like this. One couldn't be too cautious, for in Godfather's regime anything you did could get you into trouble, especially doing nothing.

I went past the cafeteria and sneaked into the library. I remember distinctly the tangy smell of refrigerant gases, which stalked the corridors of our office, slipping in with me. Judging by the stuffiness, the room wasn't opened much. I hadn't been in there for ages and neither, by the looks of it, had anybody else. 'There must be a librarian here somewhere,' I recollect thinking to myself. 'I know there's one on the rolls.'

I looked behind the fading sofa; I checked inside the cobwebbed cabinets; I climbed up to the dusty loft. But there was nobody here. Had he resigned or something? If he had, this was a cool place to hang out. Better than the crowded cafeteria. I preferred the tanginess any time to the smell of stale food. More compelling was the privacy. Sneak in some samosas and tea, and you could live here for days.

I seriously considered the option of moving my 'cubicle' to the library as I switched on the computer. Don, my boss, would never be able to find me in here. The Windows welcome music made me jump and I hurriedly turned down the volume.

I first opened The Collective's own site. I'm not sure whether this site exists today but I did take a printout of their home page and I reproduce it for you here so that you can judge my actions in the right context when you've read through this entire account.

'Capitalism is evolving,' the economic wizards tell us. 'Have patience, we're getting there.' Are we? Over the last century, Capitalism may have been work in progress but there has hardly been any *progress in work*. On the other hand, over the last thirty years, work has steadily deteriorated to mean a four-letter curse uttered with disgust every weekday morning by people who have nowhere else to go, nothing else to do.

Consider this. **One hundred per cent of the 25000 folks we surveyed in corporations across the world fantasize about an early retirement!** Only 20 per cent said they looked forward to going to work every day.

Work is the centrepiece of our lives, where we spend a large part of our waking hours. But increasingly it's a space many of us would rather not occupy. We can't call it a prison since they pay you to be locked in here; let's say it's a *gilded cage*. 'Earn. So what if you're unhappy doing it, you'll need money to spend later.' 'You have to work, think about your future.' 'Build a nest first, you can fly later.'

What's with this future payoff thing? We are forever planning, dreaming, aspiring rather than living. When we choose the future over the present we choose a dream of joy over joy itself, a thought of love over love, hopes of survival over survival. So what if our work life is hell right now? So what if the environment is getting to be hell? So what if the family makes your life hell for not being there? As long as the future looks rosy, as long as we are on a voyage, growing at x per cent, to an unknown shore, the present be damned.

Growth at all costs. But we forget the malignant cancer cell too has a single purpose - growth. And it too gallops along on a voyage, though the shore it's going to is well known. By adopting the attitude - so what if life sucks now, it'll be all right when we retire - we are sucking life out of work, and indeed out of life itself. The temple that turned into a cage long ago is fast becoming a tomb.

Funnily enough your boss thinks it's you who are out of tune with the demanding rhythms of growth. 'My guys are like guitar strings - they sound good only when they are screwed real tight.'

Why must we always tune into the firm rather than having the firm tune into us, to our rhythm? We believe the organization's context needs to centre

around us, its real owners, not dictated by some
shareholders who will never set foot in the firm. It's
this corporate algorithm which needs tuning, folks.
We have to rewrite the flawed logic of 'growth at all
costs', of future taking precedence over the present,
and of absentee landlords calling themselves the
owners of your land.

We are a guild of management professionals who
work on organizational design – structure, systems
and culture – to harmonize the new rhythms of work
life with people's aspirations. **And vice versa.**

All we are saying is: give 'work' a chance.

Let's live, not just earn a living.

Keen to ferret out as much information as I could
about the authors of the postcard, I had spent the
entire afternoon of the day I had got it, a fortnight
ago, tucked away secretly in the empty library. After
browsing their official website, the next link led
me to Human Chain, the site Pause had mentioned
earlier in the afternoon. A professor in America, if
I remember correctly, who tracked the Progress in
Work Collective published it. I got on to the home
page and searched for the Progress in Work Collective.
A few links appeared, again far less than expected. I
picked something written by the professor herself in
the January 2006 issue of Human Chain. It outlined
the genesis of a war I knew only vaguely about at the
time but one into which I was soon to be pitched. It

was a riveting read and I am sharing the entire thing with you here.

The Collective vs. The Conscience
By Professor Janus Gemini

We know the Progress in Work Collective today from reading their only public face – their world-famous quarterly publication called the Progress in Work Journal. A study conducted last year found that The Journal, as it's commonly known, has twice the number of readers than *Time* magazine and has recently overtaken the Bible as the most widely owned publication ever. Other management magazines like the *Harvard Business Review, McKinsey Quarterly* and *Psychology Today* don't even show up on the graph in such comparisons.

No one knows who heads The Collective, how it's organized, who its core members are and the rules that govern them. Except a shadowy group of shareholders who began their infiltration of The Collective's inner core around the time the latter's Imaginequiry tool was becoming wildly successful as a vital catalyst for reconciliation in post-apartheid South Africa. Many of you may recall the images on your TV sets of the hooded figures tearing copies of The Journal, heaping them together and torching them. It was a symbolic act performed by this group that called itself The Shareholders' Conscience; they further vowed at the time to destroy the only originals of The Journal lying in a library in Helsinki, resulting in it becoming the most heavily guarded building in the world.

Interestingly, in many people's opinion, it is the world that needs guarding from The Journal, because it is immensely dangerous. The concepts published in it increasingly challenge the basic constructs of capitalism – the firm and the organization.

Due to a strange quirk, all issues of The Journal have been published in the old style before computers changed the face of the industry. As you well know, they are typewritten and available only as single hard copies, photocopies of which have been reproduced freely by practitioners the world over. Collective followers like myself have tried imaging techniques to transfer The Journal into soft copy but have given up in exasperation.

The problem is that the articles lose the famous ability to shed and sprout paragraphs like they were leaves on a tree. The Collective explains this oddity by claiming that The Journal is wired not to waste energy; the reader has to be ready for the idea already for it to make sense to them. In fact, entire articles have been known to differ in the same copy of The Journal, depending on who was reading it. The first hundred photocopies are rumoured to retain this miraculous feature of the original, but as the copies get further and further away from the original, the dynamic nature disappears.

In the early nineties, after The Shareholders' Conscience realized it wouldn't be able to get past the heavy security at the library in Helsinki to destroy the original issues of the Journal, they changed tack. If they couldn't kill their ideas, they figured they would kill the authors behind them. They cracked open the secret society in 1991 through some well planted moles, killing three core members of The Collective simultaneously at a meeting. The Keeper of The Shareholders' Conscience responsible for the massacre was caught by Interpol within a week of the killing. A famous trial followed; though the Keeper got life, The Shareholders' Conscience remained largely unremorseful. The killings continued, including the alleged assassination of the original Master Craftsman of the secret society. It is said, but has never been confirmed, that every single Master Craftsman since has died at the hands of an assassin working for The Shareholders' Conscience.

And this war is only going to hot up as the temperatures on this planet rise. Unmistakably and dangerously the planet is melting, even while we argue over who's to blame. The Progress in Work Collective puts it squarely on the consumption-led growth model of the corporate world. Shareholders demanding ever-higher consumption from the customers, they contend, are responsible for creating unsustainable life styles, which are the main cause of the meltdown. In a sensational new set of papers, yet to be published, The Collective is rumoured to have gone way beyond its mandate of 'harmonizing organizational rhythms' and launched the most direct broadside yet against rapacious shareholders and the flawed capital market. Sources close to The Collective claim these are the 'ultimate secret weapon' that will save the world.

The Shareholders' Conscience on its part vows to protect the existing corporate algorithm by wiping out The Collective from the face of this earth. 'If The Collective members don't like the planet as it is, they can kiss it goodbye,' a Keeper of The Shareholders' Conscience told me over Email.

'What luck,' I remember shouting. I was about to join a secret society slated to become extinct. I clicked on an interview link of the professor in a CBS news programme and waited for the video to load. Our broadband connection was severely challenged when you played multimedia off the web, so it took ages, and when it did load, the professor's face was fuzzy and her voice was cracking, but I let it go on to see whether I could get a few lucid sound bytes from it. Professor Janus Gemini, or what I could make out of her from the tiny blurred image, was a short, grey-haired, seemingly no-nonsense lady of fifty or thereabouts. I distinctly recall a largish mole under her aquiline nose that bobbed up and down with her upper lip like a raft tossing in a stormy sea. After a while I grew tired of watching the raft and shut the link.

I remembered Pause mentioning that issues of The Journal were stacked somewhere in the library. I turned off the computer and went over to the shelves and found them at the back of the room.

I glanced through the lot. The earliest one was from January 1983. They had been painstakingly labelled. Each spine had a sticker, which gave the volume, date of publication and the articles it

contained. I noticed that the labels had been printed
out from a computer. Randomly, I read out the names
of the articles: there were popular ones like *360 degree
– Appraisals come full circle; Inward Bound: Learning from the
outdoors; Constructive Conflict – A way forward*; others were
more esoteric: *The Team Mandala: A group's spiritual journey
to a high-performing team; Work, a four-letter word… but so
is play; Deciphering Human Patterns: Escher's recursive theme*. I
decided against picking any single volume; instead I
sat back on the decrepit sofa and looked at the entire
universe that lay on the shelves. The site had said that
many such Journal libraries existed across the world,
containing the photocopy of every single volume
ever published.

Remembering my performance therapy date with
Pause in the evening, I had got up to leave. On my
way out, I ran my fingers along the spines of The
Journal; of course there was awe but there was also
a surprising hint of ownership, even though I had
received a nomination only that morning and the
prospect of being selected into The Collective was
only a twinkle in my eye. Then, just as I was about to
turn away, I remember noticing something sticking
out behind the volumes three-fourth of the way
down on the top shelf. It looked like a slim binder of
typewritten sheets. Even though I am nine feet tall
with my hands stretched above, I had to stand on
tiptoe to take it out. A glance through the typewritten
sheets confirmed the folder was somehow linked

to The Journals, maybe an appendix or abstracts of selected articles.

I read only the first page that day in the library. It was devoted to a description of something called the Share Credit principle. In essence, it rubbished the Copyright and Intellectual Property regime's viewpoint and supplanted it by a belief that knowledge is a seedling and the more it is nurtured the faster it grows. This is absolutely contrary to the thinking of the Copyright regime – that knowledge is a resource depleted by use and hence you have to pay for applying it. Words are given precedence over experience. In the Share Credit outlook, applying the knowledge is payment enough as it transforms the original seed into something much more important and useful to mankind than when it started out as a mere kernel of an idea.

It seemed like a standard page from The Journal and declared that all you had to do to use the tools in it was add your own value and share the credit with The Collective. Once you apply a tool, you are obliged to write back about your experience with it. That is payment enough for the Progress in Work Collective. These threads of discussions, updated regularly, would be published yearly for each of the People Tools that users reported back on.

I marvelled at the selflessness of the philosophy, wondering what there was in it for the authors who had conjured up a People Tool. All they got for putting their own labour into the public domain was somebody using it without even a thank you. No payment whatsoever, not even a name. What kind of motives would such a person have? Could I ever do it? Self-denial, even while an assassin stalks you? Leading a shadowy existence, when every shadow must be making you jump and each incoming call was a potential warning from The Shareholders' Conscience?

The ringing of my phone startled me, I remember. It was Pause. 'Finished?' she asked.

In the circumstances, I found her query macabre. 'Getting there,' was my reply.

'I'm coming over to your cubicle.'

I hadn't read any of the articles yet, but something told me there was more to the folder than you could judge by its innocuous cover. Strictly speaking, I shouldn't have removed it from the library but I decided to 'borrow' the folder on impulse all the same. Anyhow, what else could I have done? Who was there to get it authorized from? The Librarian had fled, leaving his beleaguered domain to the elements. I promised myself I would return the folder after a quick read. When I got back to my cubicle Pause was already there waiting for me. I stuck the folder into my portfolio and promptly forgot all about it.

I wished the Turk up in the front of the coach to Cappadocia, the Keeper, would forget about The Quiver too. He must have got my bag in the trunk searched in vain. The portfolio had been his next target but it too wouldn't satisfy him. Soon, their probing hands would reach me because that's where, in fact, The Quiver lay, nestled against my heart for safekeeping. Once they had The Quiver in their hands, they would kill me. Probably stop the coach in the countryside somewhere and take me into the dark fields. No one would hear the shot through the double-plated glass, over the idling engine of the bus. And no one would ask them why I hadn't come back with them.

I began to shiver uncontrollably. Any hope of confronting the duo was behind me now, lost in the night like the dark shapes that whizzed past my window. I was neck deep in this senseless war and I suppose I was expected to perform gallant deeds like protect The Quiver with my life. But I wasn't cut out to be a hero. Nor a martyr.

I clenched my spare kerchief in terror and decided to pray. I searched for the right words, the mantra that would save me from the dangerous Keepers. The words were important in this sort of thing, I had been told. I certainly didn't want to worsen my case by incurring the wrath of God, over and above that of the damn Turks, with a wrong prayer.

Before I hit upon the right mantra I heard shouting

from the front in Turkish, making it evident that my case *had* turned for the worse. The Turk and the wrestler must have discovered the portfolio didn't have the goods they were looking for. I started shaking like the last leaf on a tree in an autumn breeze. The time had come for me to fall. Should I just cower at the back and wait for them to come?

One thing Guruji had insisted on was to never take my eyes off the ball however awkwardly it came at me. To know and see reality, he always said, was a privilege not to be taken lightly. I got up and looked furtively over the backrest of the seat in front of me. There was a huddle on between the bowler, the captain, the umpire and a few senior fielders; they were conferring, no doubt, on how to uproot my stumps. I quickly decided not only would I have to take my eyes off their next ball but also, more importantly, I would have to ensure I got the ball's evil eye off me.

I kissed the eye pendant and looked around like a rabbit on the run. But where would I run to in a moving bus? I would have to make a last stand. There was nothing else to do. In a flash I covered the two metres to the toilet at the centre of the bus and shut myself in. You can judge how spooked I was by the Turks because despite my long-standing fear of darkness, I didn't dare switch on the light lest they find my whereabouts. I was lucky, though, for a small window at waist height did suck in enough light from outside to allow me to make out the shapes of the fittings; I sat down on the commode and prayed wordlessly. I braced myself for the knocks, deciding I wouldn't open the door, come what may. Let them break it down. I wasn't going easily.

What if they pumped in a round of bullets through the door instead? If they used a silencer, the sound could pass off as knocking on the loo door. They could declare the loo closed to passengers and later dispose my body at a secluded stop. I took off my eye pendant and held it in both hands, praying my fears wouldn't come true. The silence was agonizing.

I remembered what Pause had asked me a fortnight before, during the performance therapy session at her place: 'Do you know your death-day, Sancho?'

'Death-day? Do you know yours?' I had asked Pause as I got up to refill my glass. We, Loquacious, Pause and I, had settled down in her tiny living room in a Delhi Development Authority flat in Kalkaji. She had promised to help me think through how to write my self-appraisal for my discussion with my boss the next day. What Loquacious was doing there you would have to ask her; she had invited him. As far as I was concerned, he was intruding in our performance therapy session, like a dog in a honeymooning couple's bed.

Pause said, 'I wish I knew my death-day. Imagine if all the people knew it just like they do their birthdays.'

I knew she had said something profound I didn't understand. I took a deep breath and waited for her to throw further light on the subject, noting how deeply the smell of Malayali spices had embedded itself into her furniture and curtains.

Loquacious burst out, 'Then there would be no fear on earth!'

He had no business to butt into my therapy session. How pathetic could he get – the dog wanted to be petted by his mistress. This dog analogy fitted him perfectly because he looked like one too. A Boxer, to be specific. There were the bulbous eyes, big mouth, the multiple folds under his chin and of course the phlegmatic manner. There were other similarities too: his irritating loyalty to Pause and his direct boss, the Director General (DG he called him, never Godfather); the frustrating habit of licking a wound or weakness in another person's argument; lifting copiously from other people's garbage of ideas; and, of course, the most frustrating was his barking away needlessly at the most inopportune of times.

Why didn't Pause tell him what she always told me: 'Never miss a good chance to shut your mouth'? Encouraging this sort of nonsense only gave false hope to the perpetrator, a crime that the families of many of the contestants on popular musical talent hunts were in the dock for. If they had said shut-up-son-the-neighbours-will-think-we're-torturing-you instead of oh-what-a-wonderful-singer-my-Mishtu-is, the kid wouldn't have been humiliated brutally by judges on prime-time television.

Pause egged Loquacious on, seemingly pleased with his interruption. 'I believe that's right! What scares people most is death. The other fears are all manifestations of this mother of all fears. More precisely, not knowing *when* death will come; most people are reconciled to the fact that it will come… except the immortalists.'

How was all this related to my appraisal discussion tomorrow? We were on our second drink, it was almost 10.00 p.m., and I still had no clue how I would escape the blame for the failure of the innovation scheme last year. Despite my pathetic entreaties I didn't get any inquiries, let alone ideas, through the scheme that was supposed to be the jewel in my crown.

Seeing my sceptical look (in reality a disguise for my confusion) Pause asked me, 'When you bat, Sancho, what are you most afraid of?'

'Of getting out, of course…' Even as I said this, the fog began to clear, swept aside by the giant broom of discovery. It was as if a miracle was taking shape, a new realization was being born.

'See what I mean?' Pause asked rhetorically because she could see the answer on my face. 'If we weren't afraid of death, our aspirations and dreams would soar even higher. If I knew when I will die, till then I would be immortal!'

'Wow! If I knew when my wicket would fall, I could try those drives on the up like Sachin Tendulkar!'

'It's about making mistakes and learning, isn't it?' Loquacious asked.

'That's what the purpose of life was supposed to be, wasn't it? Ironically we are too afraid of death to live our lives fully.' She paused to let her words sink in. 'And, it's not only death. Death manifests itself in many seemingly lesser forms of fear but just as pernicious, because any fear is death in disguise. The fear of a reprimand, the fear of speaking in public, the fear of love being spurned…'

'The fear of dropping a catch, the fear of being dropped from the team, the fear of the boss's appraisal rating…'

It was as if we were uncovering these profundities with every word we spoke. Was it like this that the great truths of the universe were discovered? When they were spewed forth from the arse of some Guru, they didn't seem to have such humble beginnings. The Guru usually pretended he'd ingested some mystical ingredients from the cosmos.

'Now I understand why no one stepped up to bat in that innovation scheme I designed last year. Why my scheme was stillborn.'

'I would call it still to be born,' Pause had said generously.

'The point is everybody is afraid of Godfather.' I looked across at Loquacious, expecting him to react. He didn't. So I continued. 'They even said so. According to the design of the scheme, each new idea implemented would have got them a month's pay. The incentive was high, still no one came forward. To participate they would need to experiment, which meant making mistakes and they were scared Godfather was waiting to pull the plug on them at the first mistake they made.

'Better to hold your hand when the stakes are so high,' I remember the plant works manager explaining to me why none of his folks were interested in the scheme. Maybe if they knew their expiry date in Frozen Air, they could have played and made all the mistakes they wanted till then.'

'Your scheme would have succeeded if Godfather wasn't in the picture.'

'Or if people were on contract!' Loquacious jumped up suddenly. 'Then they would know their death-day in Frozen Air. Put them on voluntary contract for a period of say three years, which they renew periodically with mutual consent.' I had to grudgingly admit Loquacious did come up with good ideas sometimes. 'Godfather will love it, I know.'

'At least this way he won't blame me for the failure of the scheme. Thanks, I know what and how to write in my self-appraisal form. Going home now. Good night.'

Just recalling the session at Pause's place had been therapeutic; though I didn't know my death-day yet, somehow it didn't feel like it was going to come tonight, on the coach bound for Cappadocia. I was emboldened to think like this because I had been in the toilet for quite a while now and the Turks seemed to be desisting from any further acts of aggression for the moment. I wasn't yet feeling brave enough to go out and face the duo, though. The pokey loo in the coach, far from feeling like a coffin, was actually quite cosy, warmer than the rest of the bus even. Why not make it my sleeping bag?

I reached under my vest to feel the folder I was hoping would be my entry ticket into The Collective.

CHAPTER 3

The Flaw

I woke up in dreamland.

At the break of dawn, through a curtain of lightly falling snow, I saw an enchanted landscape, straight out of a snow globe. My reaction was a loud curse, though, as my first movement caused the blood to rush to various parts of my cramped body, leading to an attack of pins and needles. How long had I slept?

I let myself out of the toilet and slipped into my seat. We drove along the spine of the book of fairytales, a narrow crest rising in the middle of two valleys, which were spread out on either side like two pages. I had seen photographs of Cappadocia's unique volcanic cones in tourist brochures, touts had told me of their fabled beauty when I bought the tickets, but none of it had prepared me for what I was witnessing right now. The valley on either side was full of huge rock formations with large round bases, narrowing towards the neck, resembling more the conical caps of a clan of giants than fairy chimneys, as they were called in the brochures.

Talking of giants, where had the wrestler gone? There was a more pleasant-looking specimen in his place, probably switched at one of the night stops. About the Turk with the rasping voice, I didn't dare speculate; in any case, I would never be able to recognize him, as I had only heard his voice. Surprisingly, last night's encounter with the brutish duo didn't worry me as much today in this dreamland.

A persistent mist hung over the valley in spite of the wind. It was this wind that eroded the soft volcanic tuft to create bizarre sculptures. A flock of pigeons flew away into the distance as we passed a signboard with Lazuli written on it in Turkish and English though I still couldn't see signs of a city. Wherever I looked there were only the chimneys. From the elevation of the road, they seemed to stretch endlessly, crowding the entire valley. I searched in vain at the foot of these giant natural sculptures for signs of human life. Soon I noticed that the number of pigeons had gone up and there was certainly an increase in traffic on the road, so we had to be arriving at a city.

The coach started to slow down and then I saw it. Lazuli. It had always been there, right in front of my eyes. The fairy chimneys *were* the town. They had been hollowed out from inside and converted into houses, sometimes three floors high and interconnected from within. Windows the size of small kites peppered the cones on every floor and pigeonholes were carved out right at the top. Indeed, the entire city could have passed off as a housing colony for leprechauns or hobbits. Later I heard tales, never authenticated, that in the Star Wars films George Lucas had used just such a South Cappadocian village as the setting for the community dwellings where Luke Skywalker was born.

This was one of the only two coaches (the other was from Ankara) which came into this town. The other coach had yet to roll in, and after all the passengers dispersed the station would close for the day and reopen the next morning. South Cappadocia was quite isolated from the touristier North. And it was probably for its remoteness that The Collective had chosen this location in the middle of Anatolian Turkey.

I had read that at least eight major civilizations had come and gone in the region, as if the land were a bored mistress throwing her lovers out every few centuries. There were the Assyrians, followed by the Hittites, and then came the Persians, Romans, Byzantine Christians, Seldjuk Turks, Ottoman Turks, and finally this ostensibly secular but largely Muslim state of modern Turkey. Apart from all these, the Arabs

had raided the area often and Alexander the Great
had passed through as well. Though the population
today was mostly Muslim, at every corner there
were remarkably well-preserved churches from
the Byzantine era. Ancient trading cities from the
Assyrian days were still being discovered and Roman
and Byzantine ruins drew hordes of crowds to the
South. Most evenings, history swapped tales with the
present over a glass of wine in every village square. In
Anatolia, the citizens could never escape the feeling
that they were just minders for a future civilization
to come.

I stepped off the coach, trusting 'they' would find
me somehow. On the pavement, against the brilliant
white of the snow lay a jumble of blood-red roses,
waiting in ambush for the weary traveller. They leapt
out at me from the white and drab browns of the
landscape, waking me up in an instant. It was as if
the roses were standing in for the weak sun. In that
moment I suddenly felt alive, full of energy and ready
to face the world.

After collecting my bag and portfolio, I naturally
gravitated towards the flowers. When I got close, I
noticed a girl kneeling in the background. The most
striking thing about her was her headscarf with the
eye motif in black and white. She was dressed in jeans

and a short, snug jacket. She obviously modelled herself on the few Western tourists who came here. I estimated her to be a teenager but she surprised me by the maturity in her voice. And her perfect English. Global English.

'With compliments from The Collective,' she said as she handed me a flawless bloom. Though I smiled at her, there was a quizzical look in my eyes, which she caught.

'Things are never what they seem!' she said by way of explanation and got up. I realized she was actually a fully grown woman. And Japanese at that. I had been so sure she was a local. How could I have missed the slanting eyes? Then she took off her scarf, revealing a head of white hair piled in a bun like snow on a sloping roof. She loosened it with a shake of her head and the snow slid down and hung around her neck in silky threads.

In seconds she had transformed from an Anatolian teenager to a fifty-year-old Japanese woman!

Masuto had come ten years ago as a tourist and stayed on. She'd married the region's best-known guide, Mehmut, and together they ran the most reliable tourist agency in the area. (I came to know this later from the Grand Vizier of The Collective.) The Collective had appointed Mehmut as the liaison officer for their event and it was he who'd arranged the logistics for the entire show.

Masuto took me to have breakfast and freshen up

at a cave hotel in one of the larger fairy chimneys. It was a most unusual room with a low roof and walls hewn from volcanic rock. The giant bed, with an azure bedcover, took up more than half the floor space. A fire, lit in the quaint fireplace, added to the cosy feeling. The attached bathroom had stone walls complete with a cave drawing of sorts, though the beauty bathing on the wall certainly didn't look ancient. After my bath and a breakfast of boiled eggs, toast, cheese and olives, and lovely apple tea, I would have liked a nap in the comfortable cave room, but Masuto had said she would be waiting for me in the reception at ten to transport me to the meeting six miles away.

I smiled sheepishly at her and said, 'Amazing! How could I have mistaken you for a local flower girl?' She smiled back. Masuto was a surprise start to a day that would grow more astonishing with every turn.

Well, not exactly every turn. It took several of them along the rolling hills of Cappadocia to reach the next surprise – our meeting location. It turned out to be an underground city by the same name, Lazuli, believed to have fifteen levels, only five of which had been excavated as yet. Mehmut, the guide, who was also doubling as the driver for the Land Cruiser, was tall and dark like me, but exceptionally good-looking. He had a clean-shaven face, unlike other Turks, and wide-set eyes. I stared at his chiselled jaw and exquisitely shaped full lips as he began to explain in clipped English why the underground cities had been made.

'When the Byzantine Christians lived in this region, marauding Arab armies would come sweeping down the Anatolian plateau like an evil north wind, ravaging village after village of innocent civilians. So the Byzantines created these underground cities carved in volcanic tuft with innumerable rooms, narrow tunnels and ventilation systems. Every time the Muslim armies came the Christians would seek refuge in these underground cities along with their animals, sometimes living here for months.' Though he must have repeated this little speech a thousand times, he still made it sound conversational, as if he had made it up for my sake alone, drawing me into a dialogue in spite of my mounting worry about the selection meeting slated to start within the hour.

'How many such cities are there?' I asked.

'Well, 39 have been discovered so far. Around ten have been opened to the public, while others are too remote. Access to the five floors at Lazuli was allowed only four years ago. It is believed that many more such cities exist; in fact, ancient travellers' reports say the whole Cappadocia region was a rabbit warren with many of the cities interlinked to each other in an urban network, like an entire underground kingdom.'

'Wow! How come the rest of the world doesn't know anything about this? Must be one of the best-kept secrets.'

'The first of them was opened to tourists only in the last decade…'

'Why did The Collective choose an underground city as a location for this meeting?'

'I don't know. I am just a guide. I was asked to coordinate with the authorities to book the place exclusively for two days and a night and to receive you all and get you here.'

He stopped the car in a tiny car park beside a low rolling hillock with a huge oval hole at one end, which reminded me of a giant reclining on his elbows, his mouth opened in a massive yawn.

'You can ask *them* that question,' said Mehmut as he switched off the engine.

'Ask whom? There's nobody here!'

It was a people-less, treeless, soundless wilderness. Mehmut produced a hood in reply to my question. It was a loose slate-grey canvas affair, like an inverted cloth bag with two holes crudely cut out for the eyes. This was all getting too bizarre. When he insisted, I put it on reluctantly. Looking through the crude eyeholes, I caught my reflection in the window glass. I felt as if I were an actor in an ancient passage of rites. Or a cell commander in a modern terrorist outfit. I shouted to no one in particular, 'Why the hood?'

'Those were my orders,' Mehmut said with a shrug of his shoulders as if he agreed with the drift of my reasoning. 'You can ask him.'

A diminutive man dressed dapperly in an expensive black suit, lavender shirt, with a purple tie, and a hood similar to mine, was approaching us. I got out, clutching my portfolio for support. His black patent leather shoes squeaked on the tarmac as he came our way with strong strides. He was slim and very short, no more than five feet. I noticed his hood was an almost exact copy of the one covering my face, except it was pitch black and a little more crumpled with use.

'Welcome to Lazuli,' he rasped. Oh no! I immediately recognized the smoker's voice and the Global English accent. It was the Conscience-Keeper from the coach! The whole thing was a trap! I heard the Land Cruiser drive away. Run, Sancho, run! It was my only chance! The Turk extended his arm towards me as if to grab me. After a moment's hesitation, I clenched my fist, pivoted on the balls of my feet and was about to take off, when the suited man leapt across the six feet separating us and landed me neatly as if he were an expert rugby player.

Before I could recover from the tackle, he was already sitting on my chest pinioning my flailing arms with his legs. Then he unbuttoned my jacket and shirt, and began to feel me all over under my vest. I tried to kick him off me with my knee but he

was perched too far up on my chest. 'Relax!' he said
through his hood.

'You are tickling me!' I shouted indignantly.

He immediately withdrew his hand and asked me,
'Then tell me where it is.'

'What are you talking about?'

'The Charter, smart Sanchit!'

'How do you know my name? You are a Keeper,
aren't you?'

'Things are never what they seem.'

That's what Masuto had said! It calmed me down
a bit because she'd been right.

'You are mistaking me for someone else. You
shouldn't have hidden The Charter from me in the
coach. I didn't insist then because there were too
many people on the bus. I did come to the back to
persuade you, my Indian introvert, but you preferred
the loo to my company. Anyway, I knew we were
going to meet today.'

When I didn't respond he continued talking
without getting off me. We must have looked strange
– two hooded men at the mouth of a cave, one astride
the chest of the other, engaged in polite chat (at least
he was) as if we were sitting in a drawing room
sipping tea. 'And The Charter, I believe, was purloined
by you. So you shouldn't *act* so miffed at my attempts
to retrieve it from you. Please hand it over.'

I guessed The Charter was his name for what I
was calling The Quiver. I had read the entire folder

one evening after I got the Postcard and I knew why
he wanted it back so desperately. Deadly arrows
lay inside it, each one dipped in a poison that gets
concocted just once every century.

I think it was the day after I got the postcard, when
I had eagerly flipped through the folder with the
green spine and found a score of ideas. All of them
were typewritten like the postcard. By the time I
had finished with The Quiver (it took me around
three hours to read it twice over), I felt like I had
travelled through eternity and broken through to
the other side.

I remember thinking the ideas resembled what
in cricket we call the Unplayable Ball. Neither the
bowler nor the batsman knows it's been unleashed
because in the fraction of a second that it's in the
air it absorbs the power of invincibility from the
universe.

These arrows, too, already launched by their
writer and yet to land on their target, were in the
process of maturing their poison. You can judge for
yourself whether I overstate the case for what the
Professor on the Human Chain website had called
The Collective's ultimate secret weapon. Look out,
though, I hope you don't hurt yourself because you
might be the one this arrow is aimed at.

A Flawed God

In a period of 6 months in the year 2000, the stock of Affinity, a software global major, fell off a cliff from Rs. 3580 to Rs. 25 in the Bombay Stock Exchange. There was no significant difference in earnings or revenues or in the internal structure of the firm during the period to justify the fall.

The funny thing is, this is no aberration - stock prices bounce like yo-yos all the time. No other market behaves in this erratic fashion.

Intangibles

Two kinds of intangibles suggest themselves as reasons for such unpredictable fluctuations.

The first are the internal 'intangibles' of a company. 'They are coming out with a fabulous innovation', 'The boss is in trouble over a sexual harassment suit', 'This industry is in a general tailspin', 'The new CEO turned Grave Sons around'.

Since these items are impossible to account for quantitatively, they don't appear in a balance sheet or any other accounting document.

Second, at the macro level too, 'intangibles' influence the stock market hugely. 'This government is going to fall', 'Retail is going to open up this year', 'The monsoon will be poor', 'The euro is in trouble' - variables like political stability, policy statements, weather conditions and moods in other financial markets determine the greatest intangible of them all - investor sentiments.

Words, ahead of experience, are the major determinants of a share's price. Stories and myths abound. What do you expect? If bulls rule the share market, you'd think there would be bullshit in there.

Scams

The price mechanism is hidden behind this fog of myths to all except insiders who get to hear a yarn as it is being spun before it goes public.

We have evidence that this illegal practice is more prevalent than the odd scam one gets to hear about. *We attach proof along with this article of 25 companies where The Collective's core members have reported large-scale fixing.* It's the insider whistle-blowing on insider trading.

Though these scams we allude to are listed here for the authorities to take action against the perpetrators, the idea of this article is more to point towards a systemic flaw. A flaw which unless fixed will continue to spawn such intrigue.

The Flaw

Now price, as any good capitalist will tell you, is the main signal of a market. When this sign is shrouded in a fog, how does a market work? Con artists and inside traders abound. It's a case of one bull (shitter) leading another bull (shitter) down a blind alley, which they are making out to be an airstrip. 'Mate, this company is ready to take off! Buy as much of it as you can get your hands on.'

In the US, between 2003 and 2008 there was a $30 trillion stock market boom. Did the financial sector create $30 trillion of real economic value? When the bubble burst $40 trillion got wiped away. Did real value get destroyed?

We forget money is only valuable when linked to the real economy. Whatever goes on in the stock market would be of no concern if conmen were inflicting sting upon sting on each other. The problem is the stock price signals some messages to the *real economy,* the place where finally the rubber hits the road.

Not only is the movement of small companies obscured behind a thick fog, the big companies too get confused by the unclear signals. Take the CEO of a Fortune 500 company (whose bonus too depends on the share price) – he, it's largely a male bastion, has to land the plane on an airstrip he cannot see, hearing the divergent stories of his main shareholders on his radio, hoping one of these bull shitters is really the Air Traffic Controller he is pretending to be. Words rule over experience. And sadly, though in reality we don't come to know of it, the rubber hits the grassy patch beside the strip more often than it does the strip; of course, when it misses the airport altogether it makes news.

Is it any wonder that so many companies crash? Did you know that in 2009, only five companies remained in the exalted top 25 of the Fortune 500 list from when it was started in 1955? And that during the same period more than 75% companies exited the Fortune 500 list?

A Flawed God?

And it's not just companies, the entire planet is on skid row Because, unfortunately, the share market and its high priests have a say in almost everything we do today. At the individual level they decide how we live. What choices we make, what values we hold, what motivates us and who we relate to. At the societal level, they increasingly call the shots on macroeconomic policies, environment, media programming, and cultural mores and in a host of other spheres. Politicians, bureaucrats, as well as the ordinary person are all genuflecting to the high priests of the share market and the new God they represent. A God, as we argued earlier, whose basic algorithm is flawed.

The Tool

As a modest start in redeeming the situation, we are smithing a tool called the 'Bull Gauge', which will be attached to the Balance Sheet of a firm; a tool we hope will revolutionize reporting on company affairs. This in turn will lead to changed behaviour in the market players because once the Bull Gauge becomes law the fog shall dissipate considerably.

In a related article called 'Owners sans Ownership', we argue that in its present form the share market attracts speculators, who cannot be expected to display the accountability we require of an owner. It's like expecting a surrogate mother to bring up the child lovingly and think of its long-term welfare. Or an absentee landlord to farm responsibly. We ask whether we shouldn't be rewiring the laws governing a firm's ownership?

Meanwhile, Affinity, the firm we mention at the beginning of this article, has been pedalling a new story recently. They broke the company into two – technology and education, claiming the latter (due to the immense competition in the country) was pulling down the former. The shares are priced at Rs. 175 and Rs. 65 respectively, a far cry from the commanding heights they reached in 2000 but better than the Rs. 25 they had fallen to. Still, if they ever want to take off into the Fortune 500, they'll need a better story than that. Ever since the meltdown of the American and now European markets, Affinity's technology exports too have been hit badly and the and share price is down to Rs. 90.

```
Attached are some award-winning
scripts, which won their writers
armloads of money and now we hope shall
get them truckloads of years in prison.
```

The article went on to name 25 Fortune 500 companies whom they accused of insider trading over five years and furnished proof of this painstakingly collected by the core members of The Collective.

I recollect thinking if just these two skeletons ('A Flawed God' and 'Owners sans Ownership') tumbled out of the corporate cupboard there would be many red faces and redder necks. Imagine what would happen when a score of these unsettling ideas toppled out. I recall feeling that if The Quiver survived the attention of The Shareholders' Conscience and caught the attention of the world a fascinating battle of ideas was in the offing.

Knowing the functioning of The Collective a bit better after my research in the library the day before, I figured this had to be the only original copy of The Quiver. That knowledge made me tingle all over. I didn't know how it had reached the Frozen Air library but I wasn't going to return it just yet. My reasoning was simple: having The Quiver with me for The Collective's selection process would surely put me in a better position than my competitors. Despite Frozen Air being plunged into chaos due to the upheaval at dawn that day, I remember making up my mind to go to Turkey that night, after reading The Quiver.

I had braved too much to be parted from The Quiver now. The Turk may have me pinned to the ground but he hadn't found what he was looking for.

'Who *are* you?' I shouted at the Turk. 'And what is this… Charter as you call it?'

'Sorry! How silly! In this entire hullabaloo I forgot to introduce myself. I had meant to right at the start…' As he said this, he got up and took two steps back, allowing me to stand as well. Then he came at me with his arm extended in a replay of the scene of moments ago, just before he'd jumped me, except his suit was dirty and my ribs ached where he'd sat on them.

'Welcome to Lazuli.' I extended my arm for a normal handshake but he clutched my fingers with his own, our hands clasped like two hooks; next he slipped his fingers through mine and touched our raised middle fingers to his forehead right between the eyebrows. I followed as best I could. We reverted to the hooked clasp, using which he pulled me in towards him and finally we hugged, a little askew, his heart to mine; somehow we fitted more snugly into each other's bodies this way.

When the ritual was over, he explained, 'This little

greeting ceremony is the only way a core member can recognize another member. We change it periodically. Our own personal identities we have to keep secret, you see. Even from each other. It's best that way for all concerned. Though you are not a core member yet and still have couple of stages to cross, we believe you have already arrived. The Collective shall treat you like any other core member from now on.'

He stopped to let me react to his statement.

I didn't know what to say. 'I... I am honoured.'

'So am I. Unless, of course, if you fail to pass the final test, you will be cut off with as little ceremony as this adoption. Now for the answer to your question.' He drew himself up to his full height and announced pompously, 'I am the Expert Craftsman for the Progress in Work Collective for this zone! My zone loosely covers a broad swath of area covering the entire Middle East, Turkey, and all of Europe except the part west of Germany. It's called The Seneca zone after the famous People Tuner who lived in this region just after Christ... but of course his work transcended space and time. You might know, The Collective divides the world broadly into six zones; where you come from, the Indo-China area, is called The Mahatma zone. I don't have to introduce that inspired soul to you.'

I nodded, though I wasn't sure how the Mahatma was connected to The Collective. 'Well, all kinds of groups have co-opted Gandhi...' I began tentatively.

'True, you disbelieving dodo. He has been a great muse and one of the patron saints for The Collective too. Where others had tried force and violence, Gandhi worked his magic through the people. He abhorred violence, so he had to conjure up other People Tools to inspire a whole nation to overthrow the British. He started the Satyagraha and imaginatively extended the Boycott. The two tools are even now practised in civil protests in India and across the world, I believe.'

The Expert Craftsman took me by the arm and lightly pointed me in the direction of the hillock, towards the mouth of the cave. He continued talking as we walked the short distance. 'Now, to complete my full introduction. Most pertinently for you, I am also the Grand Vizier of this Playshop at which you are a participant with four others who've made the grade this year.'

'Just five of us?'

'The selection process is not exactly a bed of roses. The Master Craftsman is very exacting.'

'Ah, the Master Craftsman! I'm so excited I'm finally going to meet him!'

'I don't know about that. As of now you have me. You see, I have been asked to preside over the Playshop.'

We'd arrived at the mouth of the cave. From inside, rays of darkness pierced the weak sunshine like fingers trying to clutch us by our collars and pull us in. 'On the matter of The Charter...' He turned towards me.

'There's been a mistake,' I assured him. 'You have searched my bags, my portfolio and now my body. I don't have this Charter you have been going on about.'

'Hmmm... The Master Craftsman usually doesn't make a mistake. Let's take this up again at the end of the Playshop. But for your sake I hope you're not being sly about it.' He walked into the darkness with a spring in his step.

Every instinct was asking me not to follow him into the cave. There was my mortal fear of darkness, of course, but another phantom was striking terror in my heart: the opposition. How would I take on four seasoned HR professionals? The Quiver may have some of the answers; only, I would need to ask the right questions, wouldn't I? Not having studied HR in a college would be a handicap for sure.

I thought of how Guruji had manoeuvred me through Cooch Behar, past the Ranji Trophy level, into the fringes of the Indian team. Of course, I had talent, but then there was no dearth of that in a country one billion strong. It was your 'upper storey' which got you anywhere, as Guruji never tired of telling me. I had tapped his top floor through my chequered career, especially the year I turned twenty, I remember, and my batting average refused to rise past the teens. If it hadn't been for Guruji's canny strategy of demoting me down the order, I would have had to quit cricket that year. But hidden in the middle order, out of the firing line of the fieriest bowlers, I got a couple of fifties – just enough to survive the year.

Maybe that's how I needed to handle this Playshop: not open the innings, hang back, let the others do the hard work and then slip into the middle order using the advice of The Quiver as my coach.

I clutched the eye pendant tight in my fist and kissed it before letting the darkness envelope me.

CHAPTER 4

The Sting

'Hello and welcome to the coloured version of the Ku Klux Klan,' said the Grand Vizier. 'The hoods were quite a surprise, weren't they? I recall my first impressions of The Collective too were loaded with scepticism, colourful comrades. During my Induction Playshop, which by the way is what this meeting is called, I remember looking around at the multi-coloured hoods filled with wonder, curiosity, fear and the foolishness of it all. I might even have giggled. You must be feeling the same way. At the same time there must be anticipation gnawing away at your bosoms. For the moment I request you to suspend those emotions, empty your hearts and listen to me. Focus, friends, on me, your Grand Vizier, and I promise to get you through this preliminary bit, as quickly as I can before the game begins. To start with: some announcements the occasion requires, and I must rise to it.'

There were just six of us in the giant 'hall' on, what we later came to know was, Level Zero of the underground city. It was difficult to understand the Grand Vizier as his rasping words bounced off the rough rock walls and floated in slow motion, until they died. The lighting was worse than the acoustics. A source far above on our right shone like a weak torch on its last cells, producing just enough of a glow for me to keep my fear of darkness at bay. I looked around at the others to see how they were coping but I could only make out silhouettes. I couldn't even tell whether my neighbour was a man or a woman.

Peering closely now, I noticed my neighbour on my left constantly adjusting something over the hood. I shuffled back so the person was ahead and to the right of me. On deeper scrutiny, I found thick spectacles perched over my neighbour's hood. At one level, my heart bled for my neighbour because this place was difficult enough for the normal-sighted. But at another, baser level my heart was filled with a quiet satisfaction at having one less person to compete with for a position in The Collective. My neighbour would never make it with the handicap.

'This Playshop is not a competition,' the Grand Vizier announced as if he had read my mind. I noted this was not the first time he'd done that. He seemed to have a gift for it. 'There are no winners or losers here, only players. That, in a nutshell, is the message from the Master Craftsman. As all of you know I am the officiating Grand Vizier for this Playshop. The Master says: "Greetings and congratulations! Our selection criterion is very exacting, which is why you see just five of you here who've made it from more than a thousand nominations across the world. When I say 'made it', I say it with hope for there are two more legs to go – this Induction Playshop and the Final Task to be set for you at the end of this Playshop. Of course, to have arrived here is a feat you can be proud of. As you go through this Playshop, remember the biggest expectation we have of you today is to just play and enjoy it. Don't play to win… or lose for that matter. Take yourselves lightly and have fun!" That is the Master's entire message, loving listeners.' The Grand Vizier paused for emphasis. 'Any questions?'

'Yes, please, *Venerable* Vizier,' my bespectacled neighbour spoke up in a husky voice. The words 'Venerable Vizier' were enunciated with an affectation and, just for that, if I had to take a bet I would put it on my neighbour being a man. More certain was the Cockney accent and the mocking tone. He was not very tall or was it the effect from him stooping as he peered through those thick spectacles in the gloom? He wore a dark full-sleeved shirt and I could just make out the waistband of his black denim jeans. In complete contrast to the clothing was the bright green hood he wore on his head.

'As a result of all the camaraderie you are promoting, suppose two Collective members were to fall in love, what happens then? Can we see each other's faces? Or do we have to even make love wearing these blasted masks?'

There was a shocked silence at his words. The Grand Vizier made a choking noise I took to be a sign of displeasure. I began to feel sorry for my neighbour because I had experienced the animal that lurked in the Turk.

He sputtered like a generator coming to life and finally began to roar in full throttle. Only now it became clear that he was actually laughing with no holds barred. Soon his guffaws were echoing all over the 'hall', as if Ravana's ten heads lay laughing, dismembered in different corners. My opinion of him had been undergoing a quiet transformation since I had entered the cave and it turned the corner with this comment. I had started on his wrong side and now I saw the glimmer of a road leading to other parts of his personality.

The spectacled Brit giggled nervously, unsure of what his remark had started off. Someone else chuckled and then took off whooping in hoots of amusement. The rest of us couldn't help but join in. Instantly, the tension eased and the mood turned from sombre to relaxed.

As we drowned our fears and anxieties in the sea of laughter, we warmed up to each other and to the Grand Vizier. I saw a tall, barrel-chested man in a cream-coloured hood tap my neighbour good-naturedly on the back, sort of thanking him for setting us off. A woman who'd let her long black hair down (it flowed over her back, way beyond her turquoise blue hood) stamped on my foot inadvertently. My loud yowl started a rash of animal sounds; someone began to bay like a wolf and the barrel-chested man did a good imitation of a rooster. Amid the yowls and hoots, the long-haired lady tried to apologize to me but every time she tried to speak, she would dissolve into a titter. There was something so polite about the titter, like she really did want to stop. Surely Oriental. Combined with her straight silky hair and diminutive stature I placed her as a South-East Asian, maybe from Thailand or Vietnam.

We must have been in hysterics for a couple of minutes, but it was deeply therapeutic. Obviously we had all been very nervous. Strangers in an alien land, huddled together in the murky gloom of an underground city wearing those bizarre hoods, part of a secret guild we didn't know much about, we were all a long way from home.

When the meeting came back to a semblance of order, the Brit pressed his advantage. 'On a more serious note, *Vulnerable* Vizier, I do have a request. These hoods make a bad situation worse. If we have to go through this Playshop of yours wearing them, we need more lights, mate. And could you turn the damn reverb off on your voice while you're at it?'

'Sorry, miffed mate, the lights and sound are not in my control. Neither is my pompous designation. I didn't invent this title, I just inherited it but I am sure the joker who coined it hankered after just this effect. You have two choices for this entire situation – love it or lump it.'

'I don't think I really have a choice; I guess it's the latter for me,' the Brit said.

'Only for the moment, I hope. You will soon grow to love it. The Master Craftsman, you recall, emphasized on having fun as the most important criterion for this Playshop and with that collective hoot I think we are well under way. Psychiatrists study disease to come up with solutions for mental health, while we believe in studying fun to come up with wellness tools. Which is also the reason, curious comrades, we are calling this event a Playshop rather than a Workshop. We believe that when you are enjoying yourself, you're at the peak of your potential, you learn effectively and most importantly you impact people positively. Fun is infectious, it's a congenital disease all of us are born with. Unfortunately, we develop antibodies to fight fun as we grow up. In this Playshop we'll all lower our immunity to fun and along the way we'll hopefully pick up some tips to live a fuller life. Learning, by

the way, is factored into play. You don't have to make
any effort.'

'So all play and no work makes Jack clever
according to you?' My bespectacled neighbour had
taken on the mantle of spokesperson for the group.

'I didn't say that. I was hoping we could transform
work into play. Maybe we'd get less "work" done but
at least we'll learn much more.'

The Brit wasn't convinced. 'If you ask me, this
"work is play" paradigm is a bit over the top. Work
is work.'

I agreed: work was serious business. You couldn't
fool around and get by at work. In fact, I believe play
had to be approached like work if you wanted to get
anywhere nowadays. I recall the struggle and hard
work it took for me to make it into the zonal team
for the Duleep Trophy; I wouldn't have been selected
had I considered it as *just a game.*

Of course there were some, the double agents,
who pretended to be playing while they were actually
working. You couldn't tell which was which. Like Don
on the day of the upheaval at Frozen Air.

I remember I came to know about the sting that led
to the upheaval during my appraisal discussion with
Don. It was the day after the postcard landed on my
desk. On the evening before the discussion, Pause

had helped me to re-imagine the innovation scheme debacle and I had done a decent job of writing up my self-appraisal accordingly.

When I walked into his room, Don was reclining in his chair, his legs in ankle-high boots resting on his massive glass-topped table. He was looking out of the giant bay window to his left with a dreamy faraway expression. Armchair travel was his favourite pastime. He loved being all over the place without really getting anywhere specific.

'Good morning, sir,' I said loudly to attract his attention. There was a sort of echo in the large room, which I had noticed before.

'Hi,' he said looking at me blankly, no hint of recognition in his voice.

I blew my nose to make matters clearer.

'Ah, Sanchit. Good morning, boss.' His voice boomed across the room. He stood up and came round towards me and shook my hand formally. 'What can I do for you, Sanchit?'

I put my appraisal form pointedly down on his table.

'Ah, appraisal time! What fun! Sit down! Sit down! Why didn't you tell me, boss?' He picked up the form and opened it

Taking a black velvet high-backed chair, I said, 'I did. I sent out a mail along with the forms to everybody. On your behalf. You signed it, sir! And my appointment has been in your diary for a week now.'

He gave a short booming laugh. The blast caught me full in the face, making my eardrums ring like a tuning fork struck with a rubber hammer. Rubbing my ears gingerly, I looked into his eyes just a foot away from mine to figure out why he had laughed while looking through my appraisal form. They were large, wily and continuously flowing. Like butterflies they flitted from flower to flower alighting for split seconds before moving on somewhere else; he couldn't be reading so fast. Then what was the source of his mirth? I moved down to his cavernous mouth for further clues. It was no use; only his lower lip was visible under the thick black curtain of his moustache, which he claimed proudly never to have trimmed. Another short guffaw issued forth from behind the curtain as he finished flipping through my appraisal form.

'Right, let's hear it straight from the badmash's mouth. Shoot, Sanchit.'

I remember thinking I better get this moment right else the elf would be off again to another part of the enchanted woods that sprawled inside his head. I blew my nose. But before I could say anything, his secretary blew in without knocking like an ill wind.

She announced abruptly. 'MD demands your audience. Along with Mcsinki head.'

Oh no, the elf king himself beckoned. I noticed a look of amusement cross Don's face and in a jiffy he seemed to have forgotten I existed. Without a by-your-leave, transgressing a major rule of appraisal discussions (viz. 'Sit in a spot where you won't be interrupted'), he walked out of the door with mincing steps – a ballerina called away to perform in the king's court. Why had he suddenly been called away by the MD? There were matches being played behind the scenes, games I had no clue about. And Janice Kramer, the head of Mcsinki (business strategy consultants) seemed to be in the centre of it all. Masoom, Godfather's secretary, who car-pooled with me most mornings, had been unusually silent today in the car, exuding a strange mixture of elation and sorrow. He hadn't opened his mouth except once to mutter, 'Janice the menace,' and then refused to clarify his remark despite my pestering him till we reached the office.

On one of her talkative days, Masoom had told me the entire story of why Godfather had been forced to bring Mcsinki into Frozen Air. It was about a month before when we were stuck in a jam near India Gate as we waited for a passing parade, or it might have been a dignitary.

Masoom started with a fact I already knew: MD, our Managing Director, had ceded his throne to Godfather seven years before. He had been sidelined since to a titular position, mostly handling external affairs for the company. His daughter, this too I knew, had joined the ranks six years ago and had been rising up the ladder at the pace Godfather allowed her.

Things had been much simpler at the time Godfather had taken over the reins of Frozen Air. There were just three other major players producing chloro flouro carbons (refrigerant gases for ACs and refrigerators) in the country. Godfather had taken only a month to assess the situation of the competitors in the industry and play his masterstroke. Godfather's first big initiative had been to cobble together a grouping of all four companies in a cartel, and then fix the price and production quotas between the gang of four.

The cartel worked because no new entrants would set foot into our sunset industry in a hurry. 'Sunset' because our biggest contribution to society till then had been the hole in the ozone layer, but you couldn't blame the MD for choosing to set up a ref gas unit because back then climate change was a mere twinkle in the eye of faddist green activists. After our role – or should I say hole? – had received eminent attention, a treaty had been signed at the end of the last century by more than 150 countries known as the Montreal Protocol, giving our industry a decade or so to fade away into the sunset and usher in a sunrise of new, greener technologies.

But there was still some time for the sun to set on us. And it became clear that dusk would be further delayed by the glitches in the commercial viability of the new technologies. Meanwhile, global warming had ironically only increased the demand for refrigeration. So for six years, our cosy foursome had been milking the customers. The profits had rolled in; the economy had been growing like never before and the customers, not having alternatives to the gang of four, had had to swallow whatever price we would set from time to time. To explain his strategy, Godfather had once famously said in an open staff meeting. 'A cow has to be milked, else it falls ill.'

Much of this was not new to me and so I was only half listening to Masoom, keeping my eyes on the traffic. Just as we began to move, Masoom told me something that I had never heard before, though I had been feeling it in my gut for some time now. He said it was clear our cow had become too fat on the super profits of cartelization. When the grass was easy all year round and you didn't have to exercise to get it, it was natural that flab would follow.

The external context had changed dramatically too. For one, the climate change debate had heated up considerably and though the governments had yet to come to any agreement, the consumer opinion was rapidly turning green. Also, the agreed date for shifting to the new technologies was almost upon us now and we hadn't yet tied up with anybody for the technology transfer. And then there was the most immediate cause of worry: a demand slowdown across the world (while in India the market continued to grow quite nicely, in comparison), forcing developed country firms to look for greener pastures in the growing economies.

Our MD, Masoom said, had panicked at this stage and due to shareholder pressure had forced his deputy's hand to call in Mcsinki to guide our play on this tricky wicket. Their mandate was to advise the duo on the course Frozen Air should follow from here on.

'But the DG isn't very hopeful about Mcsinki. He thinks that instead of navigating us through these troubled waters they just might sink us.' Masoom alighted from the car in front of the office building.

'At least he has some hope. I am hopeless about that bugger Ram Jag,' I said, getting out from the other side of the car, referring to Godfather's personal peon. 'He would have removed the attendance register by now for sure. And the bastard won't listen to our pleading about the jam. Half day leave gone again!'

'That bloody Ram Jag!' I shouted in Don's room where I was waiting for him to come back to finish my appraisal discussion. The echo made me realize where I was. I looked around the bare room. Sparse furniture, no paintings on the wall, no books on the shelf except (surprise, surprise) Cervantes's *Don Quixote*. He knew he was called Don by some of us and must have bought the book to find out why. I got up and picked it off the shelf. Oof! It was heavy, and so was the style it was written in. I closed it and heaved it back onto the shelf.

I went around his desk and opened the most prominent drawer in a small cabinet near Don's chair. It was empty, as were the other drawers save the one at the bottom. Nestling inside it, innocuous as a stapler, was a gun.

'Oops!'

I was about to close the drawer when on a whim I picked up the pistol. I can see it almost as if it were in front of me now. It was small, like a ladies' revolver and seemed pretty old. The butt was plated with ornately carved ivory. The trigger and the safety latch were made of ivory too; the trigger was carved to resemble a hooked finger and the latch was in the shape of a thumbs up. I turned it around to see whether it was loaded but I had no clue how to open its chambers. I was looking down its barrel when I suddenly panicked. Suppose the elf decided to shoot somebody later, the gun would have my fingerprints all over it. I quickly wiped it with my kerchief, in the process adding some shine to the gun, and bent down to put it back.

Suddenly the HR Director entered the room like a bullet and hit me on the back of the head. I shot upright with the shock. 'It's on!' he boomed. Seemed like he was referring to a switch inside him, because he was beaming like a lighthouse. I closed the drawer surreptitiously with my leg and waited for him to illuminate my neck of the woods but he just kept glowing wastefully at nothing in particular.

'What's happened, sir?' I wished he'd stop grinning like an imbecile. 'What's the joke?'

'It's on the DG, the Damn Gwala.'

'What do you mean?'

'The cow's been sold. The milkman is out of a job.'

'Sold?'

'I mean bought. We've been bought by United Air.'

'The airline?'

'Sorry, I mean Unified Air.'

'What? I don't believe...'

'Sanchit, you badmash, be careful now. That's no way to start with your new masters. You better believe in them.'

'But I thought Mcsinki...'

'They sunk him, boss. It was they who stitched together the deal behind the scenes, while the foolish cowherd kept milking his cow!' He spat this out viciously. 'As per the deal with Unified, the MD's illustrious daughter Aatushi is your new CEO. He came around the table, saw the drawer open and picked up his gun. 'And the DG has been asked to Depart, Go.' He pretended to blow smoke from the barrel. Then he began to guffaw with his mouth wide open, his whole body shaking with mirth, his eyes screwed up as if in pain. I could hardly recognize him in his impersonation of the evil Joker in *Batman*. Where was the affable buffoon I knew?

There was no point in returning to my appraisal discussion after what had happened. My heart wasn't in it. I wanted to know more about the breaking news. I picked up my form and left the diminutive villain standing at the bay window, pistol in hand, cackling away at the world, oblivious to my scurried departure.

I walked out and turned right, further up towards the lobby at the end of Rajpath. I looked in on Masoom's workstation just outside Godfather's chamber. He was gone! Cleared out with all his stuff! I didn't dare look further into the lair itself and retraced my steps. Just outside the door I ran into Ram Jag, Godfather's peon, lord of the attendance register; he who had once dictated the entry and exit of all executives with an iron hand now looked ready to burst into tears. I stood silently in front of him trying not to look sympathetic.

He broke down nevertheless. Sobbing, he whispered, 'My baap. Save me!'

My tormentor's assistant needed my assistance. I suppressed my glee, trying to strike up a genuine pang of pity. It struck me back cruelly. After all, this was the man who'd whisked away the register sharp at 9.00 a.m. every morning, stealing from me numerous half-day leaves even though I had been late by only a few minutes. And I wasn't the only one. Many others would have wanted me to let him stew in his cauldron, calling it divine justice.

Purely out of curiosity, I asked him in Hindi, 'What happened?'

'What do you mean "what happened"?' A hint of the old aggression killed any scope of me softening my stance. 'They have betrayed my boss. Didn't even allow him to come and collect his things this morning. Relieved of duty from home! What a shame. After he'd given his life for the company.'

I could still hear Don's laughter ringing in my ears; the ramifications of the diabolical coup sunk in for the first time. 'Where's Masoom?'

'Masoom Bhai was asked to clear out this morning at eleven. He just left… What's going to happen to me?' The most pathetic sight in the world has to be a grown man reduced to tears, but I was unmoved. Revenge was stirring in my bosom. This man's boss (whose style Ram Jag completely endorsed and copied) had made me cry like this on more occasions than I cared to count.

'Resign like Masoom and be free of your fear,' I said but I knew at his level the stakes were too high because it wasn't easy getting alternative employment in the unskilled category in this labour-surplus economy. 'Stop crying, for God's sake!' I spat out.

He seemed alarmed at my ferocity and quietened down instantly, wiping his eyes with the back of his sleeve. The second most pathetic thing in the world has to be a grown man taking orders with such alacrity.

I melted. 'Okay, I'll help you, but reluctantly. Let me be clear. You've ruffled too many feathers. They haven't got to you yet but when the witch hunt starts in earnest, you're the first one who'll burn at the stake. Now, listen to me carefully. There's only one way to save you. I am going to get you posted to the plant starting tomorrow.' Although in Godfather's regime you had to get permission even to put a picture of your spouse in your cubicle, I figured that in the confusion, which was inevitable in the first few days of the new regime, I could swing a transfer of an underling. By the time anyone remembered him, Ram Jag, tucked out of sight, might escape the axe.

'How can I thank you?' He fell at my feet. 'My children will remember what you did, forever...'

I withdrew my feet hastily. Harshly, I said to him, 'Enough of that. Get going now. Go home and pack. Call me at five in office to get further orders.' I turned to go and then remembered something. 'By the way, get me the attendance register from Godfather's office. I want to take charge of it.'

While he went in for the register, I pondered over the sudden turn of events. Godfather's ouster, whether it turned Frozen Air around or not, could turn around my career at Frozen Air. The axing of the opposition's most ferocious bowler surely augured well for me. Of course, it would all depend on how I played my second innings. Something told me I would be able to make more of it than the first.

At the Induction Playshop in Lazuli the Brit was playing well too, taking on the Grand Vizier confidently on the front foot. 'You know what else is over the top, apart from the "work is play" paradigm? The secrecy, the hoods, and this weird underground venue – this whole Work-Playshop. Are these part and parcel of The Collective rites, worthy Vizier?'

'No. Since the Iceland incident, we hardly meet. They almost wiped out the entire second and third levels of The Collective. It's too tempting for our enemies if so many of us gather together at one place. In the early days, we used to have many such gatherings, but...'

'Can you tell us a little more about those days? About how it all started? Tell us The Collective's origin story, Wise Vizier.'

'I am sorry to keep answering all your queries in the negative, my questioning queen.'

Queen? Strange. I could have sworn the Brit's line of thinking was distinctly male. 'There are no records of how The Collective came into being or of the rules governing this guild. The Collective believes in the oral tradition. So we don't write anything down... except The Journal, which too is dynamic as you know. We believe nothing should ever be written in stone. That way you can make it up as you go along and as the circumstance demands. We have no written rules. The only documented credo is the Share Credit philosophy you are all more than familiar with and will be practising as we proceed into this Playshop.'

'Come off it, mate! There must be some tales about the source. Even if there are no scriptures, there must be an equivalent of coffee-machine folklore...' She wasn't going to let him skip through this part and get to the Playshop, which he seemed eager to do. She had my support; before we embarked on any selection exercise, we had a right to know more about the guild.

'Well, you are right there, persistent pal. All I know about how it all started is from talking to some of my predecessors. It's said a group of friends in Finland in the late seventies were very impressed by the Zapatista revolution in Mexico. What intrigued them most was the anonymity of Zapata himself. Whenever the government forces would go to a village, they would round up all the able-bodied men and ask, "Who is Zapata?" They always got the same answer: "I am Zapata." One man would get up and then another, and say, "I am Zapata," and then all the men would take up the shout, "I am Zapata." The revolution was many decades old but the troops had never found the real Zapata or even if they did they never knew it.'

He stopped to adjust his hood as if to emphasize the anonymity. 'The Finnish friends started this invisible initiative on similar lines keeping the personalities in the background and letting their good work do the speaking. Only then, they believed, would every human on earth own up to the cause – "Harmonizing people with the reality and creating rhythms for an emerging world." Our credo was simple: every person is a citizen of the world, a Zapata in her own sphere of influence.'

Personally, I didn't agree with all this diffidence. The oath of anonymity seemed old-worldly; a whole society of superheroes cowering behind an unsigned Journal when they could be inspiring the world by coming on stage and graciously accepting a standing ovation.

'In reality there was a Zapata. Like our Master Craftsman is our Zapata, right? Within the society you must know who he is. At some time the hood must come off.' The Brit was hanging in there for more clarity.

'Once a hood, always a hood, they say. You will remember, when the proverbial cat went looking curiously under the hood of the garbage can, she was killed. Likewise, a core member like you became too inquisitive and that's how our first Master Craftsman was killed. It wasn't done on purpose but the nosy

insider unveiled him to our enemies, the Keepers of
The Shareholders' Conscience. So the hoods must
NEVER come off. Do you understand?' His tone
suddenly took on the severity I had heard in it last
night in the coach. 'It's best we don't know! Nobody
is clear who the first Master Craftsman was or how
many there have been since.'

'Fine, have it your way. But please introduce us to
this... conscience of yours, if you don't mind. I'd like
to say hello before it starts getting rude.' She wasn't
the type who'd get cowed down easily.

'Sure, it'll be my pleasure. It is said that some
unknown uncles and anonymous aunties who
worship the share market have promoted The
Shareholders' Conscience. No one knows their real
identities. Right from the start they have had a one-
point programme – maintain the corporate status
quo and wipe out The Collective's agenda for change.
Murderous attacks have been their way of terrorizing
us to close shop. It is rumoured, they have vowed to
kill every core member till the guild accepts the way
the current corporate world is wired. To combat this
brutal opposition, courageous comrades, we too
have had to take extraordinary measures to protect
ourselves.' He took a deep breath as if he was getting
ready for a momentous revelation. 'To ensure The
Collective is never without a head, none of us has a
clue as to who the Master Craftsman is, but all of the
core members at the Expert level own up to being the

Chosen One, like in the Zapata legend. So if you ask me directly, I'll say I'm the Master Craftsman.' He let the words sink in. 'In the same breath let me clarify that every Expert Craftsman would say the same. The core members don't meet anymore for security reasons. This one is the only yearly meeting now, an exception because you all are yet to become core members. Later, if all goes well and you're selected into The Core Collective, you'll only communicate by phone. If we meet by chance then the only way to recognize a guild member is through the greeting, which changes periodically. And we don't own up to what we submit to The Journal via an elaborate maze of mails that are impossible to trace. The cause is paramount. Personalities don't matter. In our sky there are no suns or moons, we're all shining stars. Everybody is a hero. Each one has to stand up to become Zapata. One Zapata alone can't save six and a half billion of us.'

'But he is the first among equals…'

'No, no, you've got the wrong idea. The Master Craftsman is not the Grand Vizier of The Collective. Ours isn't a feudal structure that needs a king. Sultans need not apply here. The Master Craftsman behaves like any other foot soldier who submits people solutions to the world. Once he becomes the Master Craftsman, he doesn't hang up his boots and "manage" this guild. The guild is pretty much self-managed, without any hierarchy among the different levels. It does have levels but they are based purely on learning, my precious pupils.'

Nonsense! I had heard this rubbish spouted by Hindu godmen as well: 'We've come into this world only to learn and in each life, if we are "aware" as students, then we ascend the learning ladder to finally reach enlightenment.' Peep into any ashram and you'll experience the opposite – there is a clear power hierarchy, a feudal set-up promoted by these gurus, who sit right at the top of the heap, wallowing in the hero worship, diverting the adulation to themselves rather than the gods they supposedly represent.

I don't know what got into me. Maybe it was the Grand Vizier's emphasis on it being a friendly with no winners. I broke my resolve of not taking a risk in this early stage of the match, of not opening the batting. I walked out into the middle to partner the Brit. I suppose the Grand Vizier, by laughing at himself, had set that kind of a context.

I said tentatively, 'Most learning hierarchies do have a pecking order, though. Religion, for instance. Knowledge is power and in the religion to which I belong the high priests wield it very effectively. So I am a little sceptical when you say there is no power play between the "learning levels" here at The Collective.'

'Well, we aren't a religion. And thank God for that. Unfortunately, a section of the public is trying to promote this view but I would exhort you to discourage anybody from having these delusions. You are right when you say organized religion has bastardized these "learning hierarchies". But there it's all a game of money. Even power is finally a means to money. At The Collective, by design, there is no money involved. And I believe where there is no money there isn't too much power play either. However, I shan't try to change anyone's viewpoint here; your own experiences with The Collective will accomplish that.'

'Don't the core members aspire to climb the learning ladder to higher levels?' I asked him, knowing that status was as important a motivator as money for playing power games.

'Too much talking, lovely listeners. We need to act now but I will quickly outline the different levels at The Collective before I hand over this Playshop to you. There are four levels. If you get past the next two legs of the selection process then you start as Novice Craftsmen. Depending on the number and quality of your submissions to The Journal, within a few years you would elevate yourself to the next level of Practising Craftsmen. The third learning level is the Expert Craftsman,' and he tapped his chest, rather too proudly, I thought, for the philosophy he was espousing, 'which you arrive at based purely on how widespread the practice of the People Tools you've developed is and also the critical experiences you've had in applying them yourself. The final level – there you have me, none of us is sure about the process of getting there. Or, even if I am, I shan't be telling you how we ascend to become the Master Craftsman. All of us at the Expert level own up to the title of Master Craftsman, as I said, but there is a person who really dons that crown. This Master Craftsman chooses his successor and how it is done is unknown. Even folklore is silent about that.'

The tall, barrel-chested man adjusted his cream hood self-consciously and spoke for the first time. He had a North European accent I couldn't precisely pinpoint. Could have been Norwegian or maybe from one of the other Scandinavian countries. Anyway, his question was, 'Specifically, how do you get to the next level? Let's say a novice wants to become a... a practitioner, what does he have to do to get there?'

The Grand Vizier seemed amused. It seemed a typical query from an ambitious candidate to a selection committee. With a short laugh, he said, 'I'm sorry, maybe I forgot to clarify: actually you don't get to any of the levels, it's the levels that get to you.'

'What do you mean the level gets to you?'

'I mean the level lets you know when you're ready to get to it.'

'Can we just nominate ourselves to the higher level?' I decided the cream hood was Dutch, though I could have been wrong by a few thousand kilometres.

'No, like I said, the level nominates you. Learning,

real learning, speaks to you. You just have to be quiet and listen to its wisdom. It'll tell you whether you're ready or not.'

'I don't understand. How does it work actually?' The tall Dutchman said this very tentatively, but he needn't have been so hesitant because he was speaking for all of us. I wasn't too interested in the details he was digging for, but to me, too, the general concept was still far from clear.

Unfortunately, the Grand Vizier wasn't ready to illuminate the fuzzy gloom any further. He folded the Master Craftsman's note and, putting it away in his pocket, picked up a laptop lying by his side. Evidently this was the last question he was going to take. 'Don't worry about it. You'll understand when you're ready for it.' He laughed, but not in a superior way. 'And if you'll let it lie for now, I promise you'll be ready by the end of this Playshop. So, will you do me a favour and bring this levels business up again in our wrap-up session, if it hasn't already become clear to you by then?' He looked around now, daring anybody to ask anything further. As we swallowed our questions with large draughts of doubt, he moved on with this terse comment, 'And now, I really must cut this dialogue and initiate action. We can analyze all this till The Keepers come home but it's when we play that we really understand, my uncomprehending umbrellas. So let the games begin!'

And what a game it was. A game in which the rules were all made up and the points didn't matter. No game I've ever played, or indeed, no moment I've ever lived, before or since, has consumed me so completely.

Later, much later, to reach out to the receding Lokesh, through the gloom that seemed to forever envelope him during his stay at the sanatorium near Yosemite National Park, California, I tried to tell him the story of my adventures in Lazuli. He wasn't doing well at all and it was the doctor's idea that I should narrate something which might get to him, perk him up a bit, distract him from the decline brought on by his undiagnosed condition.

Over the years, I had toyed with the idea of putting my experiences down on paper but hadn't got around to it. Lokesh's reaction to my story firmed up my resolve to write it down immediately, lest I forget the truth myself.

At first, it took him a while to absorb his initial shock at my 'double life', as he called it; he was clearly dismayed it had all happened right under his nose and he'd smelt nothing. He made no bones about feeling hurt that I had kept the whole thing under wraps, adamantly refusing to understand that it had been part and parcel of my pact with The Collective.

Then, when I began my narration of the game at

Lazuli and had just about reached the second level, he rejected the whole thing outright as a figment of my imagination. Hooded comrades playing games in an underground city in Turkey to gain admission to a secret society was admittedly a fantastic tale but I wasn't its author, I tried to tell him. All my efforts to convince him to suspend his judgement, to let me go ahead with my tale, were in vain.

I didn't want to argue with Lokesh that evening in consideration of his delicate condition but the very next day, taking advantage of my sabbatical, I began to write down my experiences. That way, he (and others) could read my tale and believe what they wanted and I wouldn't have to bother to defend any of it.

When I was done, I held in my hands a kind of report on the Playshop. Thank heavens I wrote it down when I did, because I'm sure, before long, my memory would have failed me. And I didn't want to forget the mad, happy, poignant details of that significant, transforming episode in my life.

I didn't just stop at the 'report' though – I enjoyed my reflection on those halcyon days so much, I let the flow carry me away and at the end of it I had an entire book narrating the flow of events that marked my passage from a boy to a man.

Before putting it in your hands, on editing and reworking my manuscript, I found the fascinating Playshop at Lazuli was hogging up too much of the reader's credulity. I didn't want the book to be labelled a 'fantasy' and cast away like Lokesh had done to my tale. After all, I have other motives, too, for baring my life to you.

I settled for a compromise. Here it is. I have respected the sentiments of those of you who like a story told straight by giving you the choice of skipping the entire Lazuli Playshop. Not that what happened on my return to India wasn't as crazy as Lazuli – some would call it crazier – but it happened above ground with people whose faces I could see.

For those who enjoy the journey as much as the destination, and like to get off the main road into the alleys, I would like to direct you at this point to a separate report published as a booklet. It details how the game Karmaderie Layers panned out at Lazuli over five levels going deeper and deeper into the belly of the underground city, each level based on a re-imagined version of Maslow's hierarchy of needs. I'd urge you to read this booklet and judge for yourself whether Lokesh's reaction to my adventures at the Playshop in Lazuli wasn't a bit over the top.

PART II

PART II

CHAPTER 5

The Return

I went straight to the office from the airport. It was early. Not many people had arrived yet. I walked across the lobby to my boss's room to report my return. Don's secretary sat in the anteroom, her gaudy pink silk sari set off by a huge black bindi, large enough to eclipse her wrinkles. Well into her fifties, she was still a handsome woman and every time I saw her I was reminded of the saying '*Khandar bata rahe hain ki imarat kabhi buland thi*' (The ruins show that the monument was once magnificent). The problem was, she refused to accept the decline and continued to consider herself a giant killer (though the only thing I had seen her kill consummately was time). She dressed in deep-necked, sleeveless blouses and low-slung saris, which only served to emphasize the ravages of time on her ample ramparts.

Rumour had it that Don and she had taken numerous trips together, ostensibly on official work, but wags insisted that work was a thin veil for more amorous pursuits. When Loquacious had heard Pause and I calling my boss Don, he'd immediately taken to calling Don's secretary 'Rocinante' which was apparently the name of Don Quixote de La Mancha's horse. His explanation, 'Don loves to ride her', had produced a raised eyebrow from Pause but I liked the name. I liked the medieval tinge to it. Even more, it put me, Sancho Panza, above her in the pecking order (she was at the level of my donkey), though she far outranked me in designation at Frozen Air.

Our interaction was limited because she concentrated on providing specialized care to the top ten executives of the company. With that kind of a portfolio and her officious façade I was sort of intimidated by her, like the rest of my colleagues.

Seeing her focussed on the computer, I tiptoed past her towards Don's chamber. The muted noise of machine-gun fire and dying screams drew my attention to her screen. She was playing the latest version of Doom. That day, though, you could tell her heart wasn't in the game in front of her. The point to be noted was that she didn't have to pretend to be busy, like the rest of us.

With her abysmal output, office wags always marvelled at how she managed to get promoted every two years. Being a mere law graduate had not come in the way of her achieving a grade as senior as a much more qualified General Manager at the plant.

For some reason, Godfather had allowed the Directors free reign to give raises to and promote their personal secretaries, though he did ask for a formal written justification each time.

I had come across one such letter in her file, in which Don cited two abilities to substantiate Rocinante's promotions. The first was how well she kept secrets. I could vouch for this. For instance, if you asked her the whereabouts of Don, all you got was a lesson in protocol on how to take an appointment. 'Henceforth the other party shall seek an appointment with the Director a day in advance, which shall be availed from the Director's office in writing, failing which there is no liability on the incumbent to agree to meet the other party. In case of a delay of more than ten minutes on the part of the other party, the appointment shall stand annulled, unless informed otherwise.' Don had declared this ability to evade the truth under a veil of convoluted, serpentine lawyer-speak, an essential competency every member of the HR team should aspire to.

The second of her virtues he'd been floored by was how she, a child of the typewriter days, had acquired such facility with the computer, though I don't know what use it was put to by Don. Her skill with the computer chiefly manifested in her playing games, where, admittedly, she was among the best in the office. In the process, she'd amassed an unrivalled collection (many a jealous player had tried to hack through to her treasure trove from the intranet but she had erected an impossibly high firewall and an intricate system of passwords to protect her booty). That she never put her considerable computer skills to relevant use was not really her fault and the blame lay squarely on the occupant of the room next to her.

Before I could open the door to Don's room, Rocinante looked up from her machine. She was unusually skittish when I greeted her. Her hands jumped off the keyboard towards her bosom and she adjusted the pallu of her sari. On recognizing me, she let out a sigh that would have shamed a steam engine.

Presently her bosom began to heave. Before I could react, she suddenly wrapped her Anaconda arms around my slender waist and mumbled into my groin between sobs, 'We are his only family…'

I wriggled to escape her hold. What was going on? 'We…'? We weren't even friends, let alone family. Sure, we had exchanged greetings almost every day for the last seven years, even worked together on a few assignments. That was all. I seriously considered shouting for help. She beat me to it. Before I could open my mouth, she started to wail like a police siren.

That animal noise was the last straw. I freed myself with a desperate twist and jerk. 'What the hell are you up to?' I shouted at her above the noise.

She continued weeping inconsolably. 'We're his only family…' she repeated, gripping my right

fist this time in an iron vice. My past dealings with
her had in no way prepared me for this show of
vulnerability.

'She must be putting it on,' I concluded. You can't
blame me for my cynicism, for I had often been at the
receiving end of her manipulative ways. I knew this
woman; she was as tough as the nails she had driven
into many a coffin over the years at Frozen Air.

I said to her roughly, 'Calm down! What
happened?'

In reply, her wailing rose in volume. After much
manoeuvring, aided by the slipperiness brought
on by her tears flowing copiously over my wrists,
I managed to wriggle my hand free. I backed off,
lest she grab hold of me again. I thought of walking
away, but it seemed really churlish to leave her in this
condition. So I went around her table and sat down
opposite her.

Obviously it was Don she was referring to when
she had said something about us being his only
family. I don't know what gave her the idea. Granted
he didn't have siblings and was unmarried; granted
too that I had saved Don Quixote some hurt and
embarrassments. But I had no feelings of kinship
towards my boss. None whatsoever. I had played
the part of Sancho Panza unwillingly. Mostly, I had
stepped up to help him, motivated by an instinct for
self-preservation, knowing that left to himself he'd
jeopardize the department by tilting at windmills.

At long last, her crying subsided. I asked her, gently this time, 'What happened to him?' I tried to keep all emotion from my voice so I wouldn't set her off again.

'You don't know? Where have you been? At 5.30 p.m., on 18th February, the HR Director was whisked away against his expressed wishes to an undisclosed location without a trace.' Grief had broken through the first defences of her ramparts but the inner sanctum of the officious lawyer remained intact.

'What? What happened to him? In English please.'

'Kidnapped!'

'How?' I was stunned. 'By whom?' Who, in their right mind, would want to kidnap the buffoon?

'The dastardly event took place, as aforesaid, at 5.30 p.m. on 18th February.'

'Tell me everything you know... but cut out the lawyer-speak.'

My request was in vain because she'd probably forgotten the language I was referring to; did she speak like this to her husband and kids too?

'On the said day, the HR Director embarked for the plant from the Head Office at 10.30 p.m. and arrived there forthwith at twelve noon. His mission was to put up the new Voluntary Retirement Scheme, hereafter referred to as VRS. He called me from the plant on my official mobile phone at around 1.30 p.m. to say he had posted the VRS. Thereafter he had

changed his plans of coming back to Head Office
due to untoward circumstances.' She looked at her
inert computer screen nostalgically. Her tone (though
not her words) turned less official; there was almost
a touch of poignancy in it. 'All he would say, and
I repeat his words, was, "There's trouble brewing
here…" I detected in his voice the childish glee he
sometimes shows. Then at 5.00 p.m. on the aforesaid
day, I was later told, the aforesaid trouble boiled
over. The local Member of the Legislative Assembly,
hereafter MLA, came to the gate with two gun-toting
henchmen to meet the HR Director. He wanted to
talk about the VRS.'

The thought of the goons set her off all over again
and her face became a blubbering sponge soaked
through with a mixture of kohl and tears. I let her
cry; I needed some time to digest the news. My mind
turned to the day (a week or so before my departure
to Turkey) when I had been assigned to handle the
VRS by Aatushi, our new CEO. I had warned her in
the meeting it would stir up discontent though even
in my wildest imagination I hadn't expected it to lead
to a kidnapping.

Soon after Godfather's ouster had become public (I
remember it was late afternoon on the day of my
aborted appraisal discussion with Don) my phones

started ringing. And didn't stop till I left the office at about 10.00 p.m. I waged a lone battle all evening, answering queries from an increasingly confused staff. No official announcement of the takeover was made until the next day and Aatushi, along with the management representative of the new masters, addressed the staff only later in the week. It had been unusually hot for the first day of February and the political shenanigans had further raised the temperature. I remember sweating profusely as caller after caller inquired about the witch hunt purportedly ordered by Janice Kramer, the head of Mcsinki (who was also the management representative for Unified Air, surprise, surprise. Later, I found she was one of their largest shareholders too). I issued emphatic denials but my heart wasn't in them for I knew better.

Business was at a standstill. Nothing moved except for the rumours. I recall Pause had left after lunch, saying she was taking Loquacious to her house because he wasn't feeling too well. At lunch, the signs of his affliction had been clear to see; he didn't eat anything and was silent except to ask me if I knew of a list of 'wanted' people who were to be axed. I couldn't blame him, poor sod. When the witch hunt started, he would be among the top three on the list. If I had been in his place, I would have had a breakdown by now.

Though I told him there was nothing yet, something was brewing — I knew for sure. Rocinante's movements had been mysterious; I had seen her furtively move back and forth from Don's room to Aatushi's with papers in her hand. I hadn't expected to be a part of the witch hunting squad so I remember being surprised when I was ordered by Rocinante (glumly, I noted) to join a closed-door meeting between Aatushi, our new CEO, and Don, at noon, a few days later, about a week before my departure to Turkey.

As I entered, Aatushi was explaining to Don why rightsizing (a politically correct term for axing people) was unavoidable. By the sound of her voice she was mustering up her last reserves of patience. 'I've told you, sir, we don't have a choice in the matter.' She broke off when she saw me come in to tell me brusquely to 'Sit!' before she continued talking with Don. 'With the phasing out of the old technology, the current set of knowledge and skills will become redundant. And the new technology will require a makeover that many of the workforce may never be able to cobble together. The only way out is a Voluntary Retirement Scheme.' She had opened up the witch hunt much wider than I had thought. It wasn't restricted to Godfather's flunkies alone. This was huge. Her words sounded harsh but not menacing, I recollect thinking, unlike Godfather's. It might have been the soft eyes behind the thick square glasses that somehow mitigated the death sentence.

Don remained sullenly silent at her suggestion of the VRS, which, in practice, had become a euphemism the management used for forcing people out of the company. Consider the term. Retirement is supposed to mean stopping work at a certain age because you are too infirm to continue. When age is removed from the equation, as in the case of a VRS, then your retirement worthiness is assessed based on some other irreversible physical or mental inadequacy. You are supposed to recognize this gap yourself and tell the management about it of your own volition, without their prompting. Now who in their right minds would volunteer such information to the management even if they get a package for doing so? Who would take an incentive to commit suicide? Only a handful who feel maladjusted in the firm and have a good job or another life beckoning them elsewhere could possibly think of volunteering to retire. For the others, a job was not a trifling fancy they could stop indulging in when they pleased.

So, as had been proven in case after case, invariably people had to be cajoled to take the VRS, which made a mockery of the intent behind the scheme approved and backed by the government.

Don, the veteran, knew all this better than me. Why didn't he protest? He certainly wasn't in agreement, I could tell. Why wasn't he speaking up? His silence pressured me into voicing my opinion so early in a meeting; normally, as I said before, I prefer to float in the sea of wisdom, on the strongest-looking raft among the different opinions doing the rounds. My rashness was also probably fuelled by my recent nomination to The Collective.

'Agreed, madam: old dogs won't be able to learn new tricks so easily. But this is not the time to reinforce their redundancy. In this flux, a VRS will ruffle things up.'

'Call me Aatushi. And that's my point, Sanchit. They've been asleep for close to twenty years – Rip Van Winkles all of them. It's time they woke up. And the VRS will do the job well. If it scares them out of their slumber, then so be it.'

'Why can't we let sleeping dogs lie for a bit? This is the time to build trust between the staff and the new regime.'

'We don't have that kind of time. We've wasted too much of it already. We need to stir things up. In any case, the VRS is part of the MOU with Unified Air.'

'If you want to stir things up, why don't you relaunch the innovation scheme we had started last year? People didn't participate in it out of fear; I believe the circumstances have changed drastically. We may get some great ideas.' I remember looking over at Don for support; he was reading something on his Blackberry, seemingly tuned out of the meeting.

Aatushi's next statement made him look up with a jerk, though. 'Sanchit, don't you know? We got a great idea from your scheme on the morning I took over. I have decided to implement it already. A strategy is being made, as we speak, to break out of the cartel and to cut prices by 25 per cent as suggested by Masoom.'

'Masoom?' I looked up in shock. 'He left the company...'

'He gave the idea through your innovation scheme just before he left. Got a good reward for it too.'

Pause's prophetic words rang in my ears, 'When you know your death-day, you become immortal, fearless.' Masoom had waited till his last hour before playing his master stroke.

Aatushi continued, 'Once we cut prices we'll have a wafer-thin margin to protect. Which leaves us with no choice but to cut costs. Redundant people will have to go. Cut the flab – it's the only way to get efficient. Moreover, we've promised Unified Air we'll bring down our recurring wage costs by half within a quarter. The VRS is our only hope.'

She looked adamant. I should have been miffed by her obstinacy, but all I remember registering was how pretty she looked with her strong jaw stubbornly set. What was I to do? I looked over at Don, who was staring out of the bay window and sipping his tea like he was an English squire contemplating his garden. That settled it. If the queen-maker (he was said to have been a key strategist of the coup) was going to let her raft sink, then I wasn't about to stick my neck out in these volatile times either. It was her business – let her mind it. Let her pretty little head worry about it.

I reminded myself of Guruji's advice: 'In difficult times, it's best to give the strike to the batsman at the other end who is more confident of handling the tricky pitch.' I took a deep breath instead of saying anything more; the lemon-drop smell of refrigerant gas soothed my nerves, reminding me of the passing of an era. Soon the aromas of the new gases would replace this tangy scent.

'What do you want me to do?' I looked pointedly at Don as I said this.

It was Aatushi who replied. 'I'd like you to design the Voluntary Retirement Scheme, Sanchit,' she said formally. 'And the list of people who we may need to volunteer for it.'

'No! Don't appoint me executioner for my own colleagues.'

'It's a very difficult role and that's why I'm giving it to you. I believe you've performed outstandingly in building relationships with the people till now. So you are best placed to do this job sensitively. It's for their own good.'

No one in the top management had ever used the word outstanding to describe my performance before. Put like that, there was nothing to do but accept the job. Also, it did cross my mind that if I took on the hangman's role my own neck would be safe.

'Both of you will have to finalize the appraisal ratings quickly in that case,' I told her. The ratings, I knew, would have a significant bearing on the list. 'I know all first level appraisals are done (except mine); the final ratings from the super bosses are awaited.'

On leaving her office, I set to work almost immediately. I shut myself into a secret anteroom in Don's suite, which we normally used for such clandestine tasks. I met no one the whole day except Rocinante who supplied me with an incessant supply of tea and the final ratings from Aatushi and my boss. Knowing the job I had been given, she was extra sweet to me, procuring for me any data I asked for and a sumptuous lunch from a fancy restaurant without my asking for it.

By ten that night, the draft scheme and the list were ready and rolling off the printer. I looked at the death sentence gleaming in the tray and felt a trifle depressed at being the clerk without a voice who'd typed it out.

The saving grace was my executioner's incentive: my performance landscape had a new mountain – an 'outstanding' rating!

I could never have imagined the effect of my handiwork would be so far-reaching as to get the HR Director kidnapped and his tough-as-nails-in-many-a-coffin secretary reduced to a blubbering sponge full of tears.

I was losing my patience with her. 'Stop crying. Enough!'

Rocinante looked up at me through her tears, surprised because I had never spoken to her so firmly before. My harshness quieted her down. 'So, did boss allow this politician to come inside the plant?' I asked her.

'No, the HR Director refused to meet him.' She began looking around distractedly for something. 'Regret the break, I shall resume in a moment...' I waited eagerly for the rest of the story as she rummaged about in her bag. She drew out a tiny kerchief and blew her nose. 'It was the rogue MLA who committed the cognizable offence! He dispatched his goons to forcefully enter the plant, while he sat on a chair outside the gate.'

'Why didn't he go in himself?'

'Some facts about the aforesaid MLA may be pertinent at this juncture. One, he limps with his right leg. Two, his eyesight is very weak. Three, he is sixty-five years old. All of the above contributes to the circumstantial evidence available of his reduced physical prowess though we don't know the real reason for him not entering the plant. He has many henchmen who do his dirty work. The aforesaid two men illegally entered the gates at 5.30 p.m., crossed the shop floor and forced their way into the HR department at 5.40 p.m. A meeting of the HR Director and some workers in the Personnel Manager's office was disrupted. The dastardly duo then asked the HR Director to come out to the gate for a meeting. When the HR Director refused, he was dragged by the collar across the shop floor to the gate between 5.45 and 6.00 p.m.'

'Just like that! Where were our guards?'

'No guard was witnessed on the scene. All were confined to the guard house...'

'...with their guns between their legs? Not one of them even challenged the scoundrel?'

'This scoundrel, as you call him, is a dangerous man. He's a notorious character of the area. A charge-sheeter with fifteen murders to his credit, it is rumoured. Most of them in the trade union movement.' She broke down. 'What'll he do to our boss?' She was sobbing again.

'Tch! Don't start again. Which political party is the MLA from?'

She wiped her tears with the kerchief, opened a file and began to read. 'He began with the Congress in 1970...'

I took the hastily cobbled together file the plant Personnel Manager must have sent across last night and said, 'Mind if I read it...' From her scowl, I realized she minded very much and would rather have kept the file close to her ample chest.

I skimmed over the MLA's political career. He had started in the trade union movement at Heavy Engineering Equipment (HEE), Surajpur, with the Indian National Trade Union Congress affiliated with the Congress Party, had then switched loyalties to the

Bharatiya Janata Party (BJP)-backed Hind Mazdoor Sabha, and risen to become its general secretary of the state. During this time he had earned a reputation as a fierce, no-holds-barred warrior against management. In 1995, he'd fought and won the state elections on a BJP ticket. Thereafter, he'd won his seat several times and his crowning achievement was the post of Labour minister in the last government. He had had a chequered career dotted with scandals that were never proven conclusively until the teachers' 'job for sex' scandal. Though he fought against the Sessions Court verdict in the High Court and won, he had been forced to resign by the party. Consequently he'd turned rebel and floated a regional outfit of his own. The new party hadn't done too well, so he'd dissolved it and stood as an independent with the backing of the communists and won the last elections by a comfortable margin.

The next page provided his personal details. Large, strapping man, six feet four inches tall with a long moustache that twirled and sat on his cheeks like two jalebis – looked to me like a gatekeeper at a five-star hotel in the photograph pasted in the file. Except, his moustache was silver and the expression on his face was one of unbridled ferocity. The name RANA VIDROH BAHADUR SINGH was scrawled under it in bold capitals. Loosely translated, it meant: The Brave Revolutionary Lion.

His moustache was no doubt interesting but it was his eyes that ensnared *me*: bulging, intense, piercing right through into my soul. They had a mesmeric grasp on the moment and a faraway look into the future at the same time. I could never have expected a photo to hold me in its gaze like Rana's did.

I quickly scanned his trade union record and saw the recent feather in his cap had been the closure of his old company, Heavy Engineering Equipment, a Government of India undertaking with 60,000 workers, in the month of May 1999. Since then, he had negotiated hard with three other large private sector industries of the region and got a huge wage increase in all the cases. All the three were now well on the way to becoming BIFR (Bureau of Industrial and Financial Reconstruction) cases, stated to be in big trouble due to unviable wage costs.

'After having burnt up all his other pastures, now he's turning to smaller places like Frozen Air for the first time. That's probably why I haven't heard much of him during my visits to the plant. What are his demands?'

'No charter has been presented to the management till 8.45 a.m. on 19th February. The rascal MLA greeted the HR Director outside the gate saying, quote, "If I am not allowed to come in to meet you, then you have to come out to meet me," unquote. It is possible that the idea of kidnapping was not premeditated. In actual fact, to start with he appeared keen only on a meeting at the gate but I believe matters took a turn for the worse when he insulted the HR Director's wife.'

'He doesn't have one!'

'Yes, but as all concerned know well, boss is touchy about the issue. The HR Director lost his cool at this underhand provocation and produced a revolver from his coat pocket. This act provoked Rana into the heinous deed. On witnessing the HR Director's gun he is said to have exclaimed, and I quote, "Want to play rough, do we? Then you've got the right man." Forthwith, he clapped his hands; his men overpowered the HR Director, disarmed him and bundled him into the jeep. Then they drove off to an undisclosed destination. I have a hunch, no evidence yet, the ex-DG is behind all this.' She looked expectantly at me and when I didn't speak, she asked, 'So, Sanchit, what should be our response to this illegal confinement?'

I mumbled about wanting some more time to think and retreated into the empty corridor.

I was confused about how I was supposed to react to the news. Coming straight out of the Lazuli Playshop, I felt totally under-prepared to play another huge match so soon. What could I accomplish by jumping in? My knowledge in Industrial Relations was minimal and my experience in kidnappings bordered on zilch. Rana, by all accounts and certainly by the looks of it, was more than a match for me. Moreover, there was no motivation for sticking my neck out because, frankly, there was no love lost between Don and I and I didn't want any blood lost either.

It didn't take much time for me to conclude that my best option was to perform the vanishing trick; skipping this match altogether would involve the least pain.

I pussyfooted down a still-empty Rajpath, planning my escape. No one but Rocinante had seen me come back from my leave. I could write in to extend it, conjuring up compelling circumstances to explain my absence. I slunk cat-footed towards the lobby. It was still fifteen minutes before nine and the place was deserted; the receptionist hadn't yet come in and the peons were all probably gathered for their morning bitch in the cafeteria. Using a whitener from the receptionist's desk, I furtively erased my signature on the attendance register. No one except the hired guard saw me leave the office. I reached the car park, descending ten floors down the fire escape without encountering any other Frozen Air personnel.

As I swung my portfolio with a flourish onto the back seat, relieved at having managed to run away from the impending inferno, it hit the back door with a loud clunk. The noise surprised me. I rummaged through the portfolio and found it was the metal spray can making its presence felt.

It was all I had left to show for the momentous Playshop at Lazuli; the spray can that would facilitate my last assignment, which would seal my selection to The Collective – 'Save a human life in your own community.'

Why such a task, you may wonder. And I don't blame you, especially if you haven't yet read the Playshop report (available in a separate booklet). To give you a brief background of the whole affair, the Playshop had been designed on Maslow's hierarchy of human needs, which ascends through physiological, safety, love and self-esteem to the self-actualization needs. For the other levels you will have to read the account given in the booklet; let me focus here on our last assignment, 'saving a human life', which was supposed to initiate us on the path of self-actualization. How it would do so is best understood in the Grand Vizier's own words.

'Self-actualization in The Collective's dictionary doesn't mean delving deep into yourself; that's just self-absorption. Neither is self-actualization necessarily a spiritual journey. In my opinion finding God takes too long, is too iffy and the route isn't reliable, tired travellers. An imaginary journey to a mythical destination on an ocean of notions is either for the really gullible or the unquestioningly faithful.

'We believe there's another path to enlightenment. Let me explain. Self-actualization, by most definitions, actually means forgetting yourself, your ego, and surrendering yourself to a bigger story. The pious say God is that story but we suggest another one, more interesting and older – the story of humankind – a story which arguably precedes God and certainly started before language itself. What better way could there be of understanding yourself than by immersing yourself in the story of humanity? And what better way of engaging with humanity than to serve your fellow beings on this planet? We say: own up to your social responsibility, show true compassion, self-seekers, and you are on a short cut to self-actualization. When you lead your community into positive change, you lead yourself to Nirvana.'

'Saving a life is not the only way to serve the community,' I recall one of the participants having observed.

'You're right, and we encourage you to conduct yourself responsibly in every other way. But it's the easiest way we can measure the impact.'

Someone joked, 'Grand Vizier, can the life I save be my own?'

Memories of Lazuli flashed past my eyes, reminding me of my new identity – I was Zapata Slate now, almost a core member of The Collective; I couldn't walk away from confrontations anymore. In my new avatar as avenger of atrocities, I would have to face up to this conflict even if it wasn't of my own making. Come to think of it, in a way I was responsible. I had created the VRS that was creating such ripples in the countryside.

Leaden-footed, I dragged myself back to the fire escape and trudged up the steep stairs built, I guess, for heroes on rescue missions. Except, my mind had not taken my body into confidence before setting out on such heroics. By the third storey, the going had already got tough.

'It's bloody difficult to go against one's grain,' I observed aloud.

On the fifth floor, my gasping lungs (or was it my oxygen-starved mind?) gave up and I sat down in protest. Deep breaths of air (I was surprised at how polluted it was almost seventy-five metres up) relieved me somewhat; it still didn't feel right, though. I owed Don nothing but grief.

A lesson dawned on me (this was the case ever since Lazuli, even the most commonplace events had begun to reveal hidden lessons): 'Getting out of comfort zones is damn uncomfortable,' I shouted loudly. I didn't even have my kerchief to wipe the sweat streaming down my temples; giving up the kerchief had been one of the resolutions I had taken at Lazuli when mutiny was raging at its peak within.

But all traces of the mutiny had been vanquished by this winding stairway to hell. I would have turned back but for the damn aerosol can; it hit the railing, again tolling like a bell egging on the Zapata Slate in me. The mind's a fickle being; fuelled by fresh oxygen, the thoughts inside it turned pompous once again. Maybe this whole kidnapping episode was a test, an opportunity to finish my Final Task and thus complete my selection rites for entering The Collective. Must have been quite a fire that Lazuli had lit inside me; the embers had a way of rising from the ashes, I noticed.

But did it have to be Don's life? Couldn't it be someone more romantic? Or if that was asking for too much, considering I didn't have a love interest or at least one not stated yet, then couldn't I save a child from a towering inferno? Something more dramatic, I mean, than saving that delusional wimp of a boss. Anyhow, luckily The Collective wasn't ranking it in order of value, as far as I knew. And why think so far ahead in any case, who really knew where this stairway leads? I fervently hoped it wasn't to Rana's lair. I got up resolving to take life one step at a time.

This time I went straight to Pause's cubicle, but it was empty. Panting from my exertions I sat down on her chair to rest. Was she still on leave? She had been slated to come back to work the day before. Since I hadn't been able to contact her throughout the Turkish affair, I had no clue to her whereabouts. Maybe her father's illness had taken a turn for the worse. Now what? This was going to be impossible without Pause. I tried to call her mobile phone but it was switched off. What should I do? Reluctantly, I made my way to Loquacious's cubicle further down Rajpath, only to find he hadn't come in either. His table was so clean it seemed he had cleared out altogether. Had he got himself into trouble?

I saw Murg approaching Loquacious's cubicle stealthily, probably looking for secret treasure. I quietly sat down on the latter's chair and greeted Murg's nose creeping around the side wall of the cubicle with, 'Cluck! Cluck!'

His head popped in and his eyes grew wide with surprise.

'Aiyo, it's you, da.'

'Who were you expecting, Murg?'

'No-buddy ah.'

'What are you doing here? So far from your cabin.'

'Nothing ah.'

'Don't lie, macchi. You were snooping around, right?' Murg had had a remarkable transformation after the management had changed hands consequent to the Mcsinki sting a fortnight or so before I went to Turkey. From an erstwhile Godfather enthusiast Murg had turned his coat inside out and overnight begun sporting the emblem of the new masters.

'I was jus' delivering da. One yenvelope I took from peon for him yesterday. Yevry time I come to his cabin da, he ees naat yavailable.'

'Give it to me!' I said roughly. What business did he have of intercepting Loquacious's mail? He quietly handed me an internal envelope with the Frozen Air logo on it and slunk back to his own seat.

I took the missive and made my way down the corridor towards my own cubicle. I realized I felt quite lost in this office without Pause and Loquacious. On an impulse, I walked past my seat (and a confused Murg), cutting across to Janpath. I strolled right till the end, past the cafeteria, and opened the library door, thinking I would read the letter in the privacy of the library. The concentrated lemon-drop smell restored a sense of normalcy in me.

Only for a moment, though, because when my eyes had got used to the dim lighting, what I saw threw me off. Loquacious and Pause sat side-by-side, holding hands on the sofa opposite the cabinet with The Journal. I didn't actually see them holding hands, because I got only a side view but from the way Pause withdrew her hand from the sofa and drew away from Loquacious when she saw me, I suspected that's what they'd been doing. I looked fiercely at Loquacious who, I was sure, must have played the pity card again. Or maybe his wicket *had* really tumbled. I pointedly sat down in between the two, forcing them to shift apart.

'Everything okay? How's Jack Daniels?' I turned to Pause, ignoring Loquacious's feeble greeting.

'Recovering. Still in hospital.'

'Oh, I'm sorry to hear that.'

'He's fine.' She said this with a frown on her face.

'And why would your face be so dark at this outcome?'

'Nothing to do with my father.'

'Then what? Mourning for the kidnapped Don?'

'We need to talk... we'll get to Don by and by. First tell me why didn't you keep in touch?'

Just like a woman to be on the offensive when rightfully she should be explaining why she had been holding hands with Loquacious a few moments back. 'I... I dialled once but your mobile phone was switched off.'

'I am sure you *tried* but why didn't you keep in touch?'

I decided to be truthful. 'Believe me, I thought of you... you guys every moment.'

It cheered her up. She didn't ask about my trip, where I had been and what had kept me from calling her. I looked squarely at Loquacious.

He tried to avoid my eyes; I discerned a hunted look in his own. He was unshaven and his clothes were crumpled. My eyes roamed the room and I began to see telltale signs of his residence in the library; a half-eaten burger from the cafeteria, numerous books extracted from the shelves and some files lay strewn around. 'Have you moved in here?' I asked him.

'No, I just slept here the last couple of nights.'

'Why? So much in love with the office or what? Can't get enough of it now that you might be asked to leave...'

Pause said sternly, 'Not funny, Sancho. Loquacious is still spending very anxious moments on that count and you would be too if you were in his position. Don't spoil it further with your crude sense of humour.'

'And how do you get news here; for instance, about Don's kidnapping?'

'Oh, I have friends and admirers who visit me from time to time.' He pointed at us.

'Thank you for including me in your list of disciples, Library Baba.' I saluted, nearly poking myself in the eye with the envelope. 'Ah, and it's my privilege to hand over this communication from the yonder world to you.'

I have to be honest and tell you it was a pleasure to see Loquacious's face cloud over. I was still smarting from the sight that had greeted me on my arrival into the library. The saving grace had been Pause drawing away from him on my entry. Loquacious's hands trembled as he took the envelope from me.

'It's a Frozen Air envelope, marked Personal and Confidential. Oh God! ' He looked at Pause. 'My name is scrawled by hand... is it Rocinante's handwriting?'

I looked over his shoulder and said, 'That's unmistakably Don's own hand.'

'No! You think it's my termination letter? Can he do that? Dismiss me without a personal audience...'

'Open it, Loquacious. Stop babbling.' Pause cut him short with a roughness I was happy to note. The sooner she shed her mothering attitude towards him, the better it was for him. And me.

'The letter is written in Don's hand too. "Dear Lokesh, I have to see you on a matter of utmost urgency concerning one of your close friends. So find me wherever I am with utmost haste. It is a matter of life and death. Regards, HR Director." It's signed by him. There's a P.S.: "I urge you to treat this affair with the utmost secrecy. Swallow this note after you've read it and under no circumstance vomit the contents out before anybody else."' That was expecting too much from Loquacious; he couldn't digest a spam text without a burp.

I was disappointed to see him visibly relieved. 'Why are you looking so happy?'

'I've escaped the guillotine at least.'

He was right. It was my neck on the block now. Obviously Don had something on me. Did he know of my involvement with The Collective? Or was it something even more sinister?

Pause dismissed the letter from the conversation by suggesting, 'We should go to the plant. All the action is there.'

'Can't we all just quit the company instead? We'll find other jobs soon. Or we could start our own

company...' Not surprisingly, Loquacious wanted
out. Hearing him my courage too wavered. I was a
fledgling convert, after all. It sounded tempting to
leave Don, Rana and The Collective behind. We could
start a new life somewhere else, just the three of us.

'What action? The kidnapping is none of our
business.' I clarified my position to Pause.

'I meant the VRS. It's all happening in Surajpur.'

'The VRS is certainly not happening. Not after the
kidnapping.'

'That's my point. The architects of the scheme
should be there to ensure it is.'

'Well, if you're referring to me, I opposed the
idea right from the start. I said so to Aatushi in our
meetings before I went on leave. Maybe I wasn't
assertive enough. This VRS is the root of the entire
problem. It sucks, huh?'

Pause glanced at me and said, 'No, Sancho, it isn't
the VRS. It's very much needed. I think it's the way it
has been imposed that sucks.'

'Well, we could hardly have asked the staff before
announcing it. They would surely have rejected it.'

'The effect is much the same now. If there had been
debate on it earlier, maybe the rejection wouldn't
have been quite so unequivocal. And violent...'

'What do you mean?'

'Ownership. It's all about ownership. By announcing
the VRS unilaterally, the new management has shown
that they aren't going to stand by their staff. So why

should the staff commit themselves to Unified Air? The ownership of the company has passed straight from Godfather to the new management. And I, in my naivety, had hoped we, the people, could start reclaiming some of it.'

'So, what are you going to do about this VRS affair? Or are you just going to blame the HR department and Unified Air management and leave it to them to sort it out?'

'Certainly not. In fact, some of us are having a meeting at noon on this topic. Do you want to join our discussion, Sancho?'

'No, I think I'll sniff around a bit on the phone. I believe the solution to this imbroglio lies at the plant, as you said. We'll have to go there anyway.'

'I agree with you.'

'The earlier the better. Why not tonight itself? We can spend the day nosing around, stay over at the guest house and come back by tomorrow evening. What do you think, Loquacious? We can have a relaxed drink in the guest house tonight.'

'I really have no opinion on the matter. Or on any other matter at the moment. I'll follow you guys wherever you go.' Loquacious without an opinion?

Thinking back on those days now, when I write this account, I feel that the shock of Godfather's ignominious exit must have shaken him to his very foundations. Somewhere deep inside, his circuitry was getting rewired for the great depression to come;

the fugitive cameo in the library was the first act of
Lokesh's impending tragedy. In the light of how it all
turned out, we should have been more mindful of his
descent. But there were other priorities jostling for
our attention. I closed the conversation in the library
by saying, 'Good, then let's all go to the plant tonight
in my car. I'll come and pick you up from Kalkaji
around 7.00 p.m., Pause. Then we'll catch Loquacious
at the Nizamuddin Bridge at half past. All right?'

Chapter 6

The Interlude

Through the hot February morning (it was too early in the season for the building's air conditioner to be switched on), there were confusing reports about Don's status. A call at eleven, ostensibly from the plant's guard room, claiming he had been released, turned out to be a hoax. At noon a letter addressed to Aatushi arrived at the plant. It was from Rana Vidroh Bahadur Singh, asking for the VRS to be withdrawn with immediate effect. There was no mention of Don.

The police had been informed about his abduction but they refused to treat it as a case of kidnapping, agreeing only to file a missing person report. Rana Vidroh Bahadur Singh had got to them before us. I speak figuratively because in actual fact he had always been there, residing permanently in the hearts of all the citizens of the area; such was his reputation that people who had never met him would act on his behalf, protect his name, die for his whim; anything, as long as they didn't get into his bad books.

In the course of my visits I had made a number of friends at the plant. It was to them, rather than my colleagues in the Personnel Department, that I turned now to explore a line of action I could recommend to Aatushi, who was sure to summon me soon.

Ram Jag, Godfather's peon, whom I had transferred to the plant on the day of the regime change, proved invaluable in my explorations. While at the Head Office, he had made influential friends in the union at the plant. He hooked me up with the President, whom he had helped out of a tight corner during Godfather's reign. I hardly knew him, since union affairs had always been dealt with by Don and the plant's Personnel Department, but he was said to be an honest sort. After the greetings, I asked him, 'So, what's your position on all this?'

The big Sikh replied, 'No possession left. *Loot litta. Assi kuda*, dirt. Swept aside by that blasted Rana.'

I switched to Hindi. 'What's the union planning to do?'

'What *kuda* do? Lie quietly in dustbin. By napping the HR Director, he has hijack our agenda *and* the chief negotiator. What *you* planning to do?'

'What's the mood like there?'

'He capture all in dustbin and key *faik ditti. Sab nu hila ditta* but *ki karan*? Helpless. DG's time too, company *vich aana chayida hai* but DG strong. No entry.'

'Do you believe the DG is behind Rana now, as some people are saying?'

'*Ram Jag di* wishful *soch haigi! Yeh* rumour *unane udaya haiga.*'

'So all our fates are to be decided by an external leader who hasn't set foot in our plant, someone the workers know only by reputation! Are we just going to stand and watch?' My question was as much for myself as for him.

'Yes. *Assi to dekhange.* You engage Rana now. *Dekhan ki karde ho tussi.* Withdraw VRS or no, pay ransom *agar boss sahi salamat vapas chayida hai.*'

'You mean money?'

'Or kursi. State Labour Minister *di kursi Rana nu vapas chayidi hai.* But tussi keeping *dhyan* – give him his want and you make kidnapping an alternative to collective bargaining.'

'Well, the way collective bargaining is conducted these days, I don't know which is worse... how can you help us get out of this mess?'

'Only Gawd can help you.'

'But... do you want to be treated like dirt?'

'Better life than dirt. *Dost, tussi bhi dhyan se. Surajpur vich ik kahavat hai: jo Rana se panga leta hai voh ya to pagal hai ya use khudkhushi pyari hai. Sardarji ki jana tussi ho kaun?*' As far as I understood the saying, it went something like this: 'Anyone who picks a fight with Rana is either a crank or a suicide case.' Beyond this dire warning the Union President had no further insights to offer. He kept repeating this caution in different ways. 'Hangman come house for high tea, you pay high price.' Or '*Tussi mixie vich ungal dali te* finger cutting, chopping, grinding only *na*?'

I had to cut him short when a note from Aatushi's secretary landed on my desk. It was a summons to the new CEO's office.

As expected, I found the short, grey-haired Mcsinki head, Janice Kramer, in the room but I was stunned to see Pause there too. So this was the 'meeting at noon' she'd asked me to join.

They wanted my assessment of the situation and whether I had any further information on the matter. I shared all my conversations with them, reporting the one with the Union President in its entirety. I ended with his warning. 'Only a crank or a suicide case will dare take on Rana.'

There was a respectful silence when I finished, which was broken by Pause, who said mischievously, 'Schumacher – the philosopher, not the Formula 1 champion – has called the crank a marvellous piece of small technology with which you can lift weights many times its size.'

'Careful, though, Rana is a real heavyweight.'

'The right kind of crank can lift anything,' she said coolly.

'So what do you suggest we do? Pick a quarrel with Rana on his own turf?' I blurted out.

The American too was spoiling for a fight. 'Why not, Sanshit?'

I winced at the way she pronounced my name. Before I could answer her query, Pause turned on her. 'Janice, darling, there are 206 reasons for being circumspect.'

'Two hundred and six?' Janice asked scornfully.

'That's the number of bones in Sancho's body. I've no doubt Rana's capable of breaking every one of them.'

'Do you know he has fifteen murder cases pending against him?' I added, hoping this input would seal all this nonsense of taking on Rana as if he were a mere class bully.

'Pause, you just said you didn't mind being a crank. What were you trying to suggest?' Aatushi asked.

'Dialogue. Only a dialogue can help us gather the information we need to build our crank.'

'You have a point. We should open a conversation with him.'

'Are you crazy? You can't talk to a gun.' Being the only man in the room, I felt obliged to explain the meaning of violence to these innocent ladies.

'Don't worry,' Aatushi said, looking at me contemptuously, as if the others weren't anxious at all. 'They say an elephant has two sets of teeth – one for showing off and the other for eating. I am not scared of Rana's dangerous looking tusks. Also, we can use the MD's contacts to put pressure on him to lay off the heavy stuff.'

'Fear is virtual; it is in your own mind,' Pause added. 'Rana has to do nothing. His reputation is enough for people to give in to his extortion.'

'What do you mean "do nothing"? He's already kidnapped one of our directors!' I clenched my fists as a drop of sweat from my underarms trickled down my side.

'Mere bluff, he was just collecting negotiating collateral. I say, let's call his bluff.'

'What about those fifteen murders under his belt?' I protested, loudly this time.

Aatushi piped up. 'Oh, that's a myth! Created by his goons. My dad's sources told me there were probably one or two cases where he was involved though none were ever proven in court. He was only obliquely implicated in the others. They said his reputation was such that when nobody owned up to a killing in the region, it was added to the notches on Rana's gun. More worrying to me than his "murders" are his legendary sexual escapades. There was a case that went on for a long time, something called the teachers' "jobs for sex" scandal, due to which he had to resign as Labour Minister though he was exonerated after all the witnesses turned hostile. But that was long ago, when he was much younger. I see no danger in talking to him. Let's sniff him out, as Pause says.'

'You are going to talk to Rana Vidroh Bahadur Singh?' I gulped as I asked her the question. By now my face too had broken out in a sweat. Thankfully the others were perspiring too though not as copiously as I was.

'No. You are,' Pause replied for her.

I was aghast. My instincts were shouting for me to skip the match and here she was asking me to open the batting against a murderous bowler. My hands went instinctively to my pocket for a kerchief but drew a blank. I looked at Pause fiercely and thought to myself, 'What's her game? Has she caught on to me? Is she using Rana as a ruse to get me out early?'

I had to scotch their move before it built up any further. 'You are crazy! I meet Rana?'

'Me too,' Pause smiled. 'And the HR Director. We'll insist he join us for talks. Can you arrange it?'

'No!' I glanced over at Aatushi. Was that a look of scorn on her face? Janice, too, looked disappointed. Pause had me on the mat. Alone, I might have been able to resist her advances, but in front of both my new masters I would have to be careful. After all, they might decide to reconsider my 'Outstanding' rating on grounds of cowardice. Better than an outright denial was to try and fob her off by being non-committal. So I sighed and said, 'I don't know…'

'It's agreed then,' Pause said to the others.

'Whoa. Not so fast. I didn't…'

'C'mon, Sancho, be a man!' Aatushi's taunt settled the issue. I scowled at Pause and nodded at Aatushi. I was sweating profusely now. 'Good. I'll put pressure through Dad on Rana while you all open talks with him.'

'What about me?' Janice butted in. She wasn't going to be left out of a brawl if she could help it.

Pause put her in her place. 'You sit here looking pretty. There's been enough trouble on your account already.'

They looked daggers at each other. The American's nostrils flared and the mole on her upper lip bobbed up and down. What was the tension between them? Things were about to turn ugly, I could sense. Aatushi, too, saw where it was going and headed it off, 'I think I need a pedestal fan in here. Or should we ask the building janitor to put the AC on?'

'Yeah! It's getting pretty hot,' the American agreed, wiping her brow.

'Janice, Pause is right. Let's not expose you to Rana yet.'

Reluctantly, the American let it go. Up close, she looked handsome. A strong nose, chiselled chin, blue eyes, salt-and-pepper hair and that prominent mole on her upper lip. She reminded me of someone... Who? Suddenly I became aware that everyone was staring at me staring at Janice Kramer. Embarrassed, I turned my head quickly towards Pause.

'Look, let's get to the plant first. Tomorrow we'll see...'

'No, tonight. Tomorrow we have to rewire the VRS.'

'Rewire the VRS?'

'I'll tell you about that later. We have a plan.' She looked at the other two women.

The American shook her grey head vehemently and said, 'They have a plan. Count me out.' Again I was struck by the familiarity of her face. Where had I seen her before?

'I'm not really counting on you,' Pause said coldly. Then she turned to me and said, 'On you I am.' Her expression became very soft as she looked at me squarely and though she didn't actually flutter her eyelids, the gesture would have gone well with the tone of her request. 'Please, Sancho, arrange a meeting with Rana Vidroh Bahadur Singh tonight.'

'You're being really pushy... anyway, I'll try...'

'Thanks, Sancho.' Aatushi smiled at me. 'It's good to have you on board. Could you get someone to do something about the heat, please?'

I dialled Ram Jag from my direct line, asking him to cajole the Union President to set up our dialogue with Rana Vidroh Bahadur Singh, whom the President knew as a peer from the trade union movement. If I had directly requested the President, he would have refused outright. My conversation with him in the morning had clearly evinced his resolve of not getting entangled with Rana. It must have taken a lot of convincing (and arm-twisting too, I later found) for him to shift his stance because Ram Jag only got back to me at four in the afternoon. All through the day I kept my fingers crossed, hoping the President wouldn't agree to swing the meeting, but when Ram Jag called it was to say that everything was arranged. On our way from Delhi to the plant, we were to veer off on to a small road along the Surajpur canal, which would take us to Rana Vidroh Bahadur Singh's 'farmhouse'. The Union President himself would wait for us at the turn at about nine tonight.

On my way to Kalkaji to pick up Pause that evening from her apartment, my hands clutched the wheel with all the force I could muster. My heart beat like a tribal drum while my nerves danced a kind of jitterbug to its tune. It had been a very warm day but now, after the sun had set, a sprightly wind had sprung up. The leaves were swirling around in the gutters on the side of the street. It looked as if a storm was brewing. Quite appropriate, I thought. It would be the right backdrop for our little act of madness: entering the lion's den. Why was I doing it? I blamed Pause squarely for pushing me into this mess. I would get even with her soon.

Standing outside her top-floor apartment in the gathering dusk, I angrily jabbed at the bell. It stirred things up somewhere deep inside the bowels of the flat. I kept my finger pressed down. It gave me the feeling of screaming at Pause.

'The bell's jammed,' she shouted as she opened the door. When she saw it was my finger that was pressing it down, she pouted and said, 'My... aren't we angry?' She was wearing jeans and a printed tee-shirt, her favourite clothes when she was not at work.

I scowled and brushed past her in a huff and sat down under the only window in the room. I raised my arms, caught the grill of the window behind me and shook it as hard as I could.

She didn't need to ask why I was annoyed. 'I'm sorry about this afternoon in Aatushi's room. I wasn't sensitive to your...'

'Confusion,' I blurted out before she labelled it something humiliating.

'Confusion?'

'Yeah. Why didn't you tell me you were so cosy with Aatushi?'

'Oh, I should have told you earlier. I spent a good deal of time with her yesterday too. She's been asking me to advise her on the VRS and its fallout for some time now.'

'How come? Why you?'

'Well, keep this to yourself: Aatushi and I shared a room at campus and we've remained pretty thick friends since. I don't like to speak about it for obvious reasons.'

I was stunned. My anger was gone. Exploring the ramifications of this new revelation, I said, 'Sleeping with the boss's daughter... So, were you in the thick of the takeover?'

When she nodded apologetically, I burst out, 'Why didn't you tell us? All along you were playing dumb about Loquacious's status while...'

'No, I didn't know anything about that. The VRS process and the scheme has been shared with me; I still have no clue about the list of "volunteers".'

She came and sat beside me and said, 'Don't be angry with me, Sancho. We all have our secrets and it's best they are revealed when the time is ripe.' I turned my head slowly to look directly at her. Was she onto mine? I peered into her eyes looking for an answer but instead found more riddles swimming in there.

'In any case, love feeds on enigma,' she said.

Love? Had I heard right? She was so close I could smell her body through the ubiquitous odour of Kerala spices that had seeped into the walls of her house. I drew the fragrance deep into my mind. At its core, I detected the tangy lemon smell she wore like a badge. But it was masked by another heavy aroma I couldn't define.

'You smell lovely.'

'It's the stew I have put on the gas.'

'No, I can't describe it. The closest I can think of is the smell of first rain on parched earth.'

'It's raining, buddhu!' she shouted, looking out of the window. 'I better get my clothes from the terrace.'

I followed her out of her apartment, up the stairs and onto the roof of the apartment block. Bursting through the door, she went straight to the clothes billowing in the wind on a small line strung across two water tanks. It was almost dark because of the sudden cloudburst. I hesitated for a split second before going out in the lashing rain. I looked around the cramped roof and found it to be surprisingly clean. I had never been up here before. I could make out Pause had claimed this common space by the number of potted plants lined up near the railing. The wind had toppled over one of the taller ones, a frangipani, and I went across to set it upright.

When I got to the line, I couldn't see Pause. By now I was totally wet. So were the clothes I was picking off the line. In a bid to get the seemingly futile job over quickly, I went for the last plain indigo bedsheet (I noticed there was no clothes peg) with my arms outstretched in front of me. As I couldn't see anything due to the failing light and the armload of clothes in my hands, I decided to pick out one side of the sheet with my fingers, and then pull it off the line towards me. My searching fingers found other fingers. Pause seemed to have had the same idea as me from the other side of the sheet. Suddenly her fingers closed around mine and she tugged me in. We found ourselves hugging each other, with a giant ball of clothes between us.

We were both laughing now. I tried to pull away but our fingers were locked in. I tugged again and this time she came along with all her clothes into my arms. I would have fallen backwards if the bedsheet hadn't still been strung on the clothesline. I was leaning backwards precariously, with her leaning heavily on me, the clothes between us, when the inevitable happened. The line broke and I hit the ground surprisingly lightly. I lay there with the clothes and Pause on top of me. I noticed the rain had slowed down to a drizzle around us. My heart was beating at this sudden turn of events. Was it just a fun rough-and-tumble under the bedsheet or was there more to it?

She made the next move. Without getting up, she began to remove the clothes from between us. Slowly we came closer to each other. One by one she slipped the clothes out and piled them neatly by our side. The indigo bedsheet had pinioned my arms in so I couldn't really help her.

Soon I felt the contours of her body and after that I couldn't keep still; I desperately searched for the edges of the bedsheet and eagerly pulled at it, tearing it in the process.

'I am coming to you. Be patient,' Pause whispered.

Finally there was just the layer of clothes we were wearing between us.

'You are shivering!' She embraced me in an effort to warm me up. I put my arms around her hesitantly. I felt her body snuggle up to me.

I wished my body would stop trembling like I was a virgin being taught the ropes in this new game. Which, to be honest, I was. Not that I hadn't had my share of women; but somehow had never got around to going all the way. Might as well admit it, I had never been able to make the final commitment. I had always believed the relationship between a man and a woman changed forever once they made love. Should I bring it up with Pause?

Before I could say anything and spoil the moment, she placed her lips on mine. 'Open your teeth, for God's sake, Sancho,' she mumbled.

I complied, happy to let her lead. Her tongue conquered me by its sensuous probing into the recesses of my mind. Her kiss seemed to go on forever. My head began ringing from the lack of oxygen. It was a familiar ring. My phone! I slipped my hand between us to take it out of my pocket to silence the instrument but couldn't help taking a look out of habit to see who it was.

'Loquacious! Waiting for us at the bridge!' I muttered under my breath.

'And Rana in his den!' She replied with a mock shiver.

Somehow the danger added to the thrill of this prelude. Tonight, Rana was the final act. Everything before it was foreplay.

This realization led to a sense of freedom from all my past modes of thinking about love. I noticed my body was calm now. The wind too had died. The night had turned suddenly still as if the sky was watching what I would do next. Emboldened by her kiss, I slipped my hands under her shirt to feel her back. I was relieved to note she wore no bra because unclasping that medieval instrument of torture always tangled me up in knots. My right hand came around, still inside her tee-shirt, and cupped one of her breasts. It was impossibly small.

A full moon, surprisingly high in the horizon for that time of the evening, appeared from behind a cloud bathing us in a ghostly light. On a whim, I decided to remove the last layer of clothing between us. I lifted and whisked off her shirt. The sight of her flawless back made me break out in goose bumps. There wasn't a single blemish on that satin stretch of skin the colour of a bamboo stem.

She lifted her face to look at me. Silhouetted against the full moon, her hair seemed to have trapped the moonlight suffusing her with an ethereal energy. She unbuttoned my shirt as she lay on me but left it on to protect my back from the rough concrete floor. As her fingertips caressed my chest, a wave of vitality surged through me. I embraced her with a vigour I had never known. Her moist breasts pressed into mine and our bodies melted into each other.

I saw the missed calls (seven of them) from Loquacious while Pause had a quick shower. I called him back and told him I had got delayed because I was losing my virginity. Why lie, when I knew he wouldn't believe the truth anyway.

'Sure, sure, the world survives on hope, Sancho. But let me tell you what I've really lost. My patience. First I wait for you guys for four days to come back from whatever important business you left for. Then you come back and jump straight into a meeting with Rana Vidroh Bahadur Singh. And now you leave me hanging around on the road half an hour past the time we fixed up to meet at the Nizamuddin Bridge... And why isn't Pause picking up her phone either?'

'I picked her up, Loquacious.' Maybe someday I would tell him the entire story. 'We will come soon.'

Pause was ready to leave. 'Do you want to have a bite?' She came out looking and smelling like a freshly prepared dish herself.

'Of what?' I said licking my lips.

'Enough of that for now. We have a lot on our plates.'

'There's burnt stew, I know. What else?'

'Malabar parotas and jam.'

'I'm always game for your parotas even if it's with jam. Why don't we pack some? That way we won't have to stop to eat. We're already pretty late. Loquacious is fuming!'

'I know, I got several missed calls from him, too. I'll just take a couple of minutes more.'

She was back in less than that. 'Ready?' I asked her. When she nodded, I said, 'Rana Vidroh Bahadur Singh, ready or not, here we come!'

CHAPTER 7

The Escape

Opposite the Delhi–Noida–Delhi flyover, on the side of the Ring Road, stood a clutch of bare silk-cotton trees. A week back, they had celebrated the early spring resplendently dressed in red semal flowers. Now the party was over, the red flowers lay on the streets like scattered baubles of jewellery and the silk-cottons stretched their arms, yawning under a full moon, undressed and ready for bed.

The party had shifted to the Shiva temple at the end of the road. It had been decked up as colourfully as the silk-cotton for Shivratri. Being stuck in the heavy traffic in front of the temple, I gave the decorations a quick glance.

'Fifteen minutes of fame,' I blurted out.

'Huh?' Pause didn't seem interested.

It was only February but it felt like April despite the recent rain out there in the middle of the exhaust fumes from the crawling traffic. I rolled up the windows and switched on the air conditioner.

'Everyone hankers for their fifteen minutes of fame. It's the temple today, a week back it was the semal trees,' I explained. 'I'd much rather have fifteen minutes of real love,' I said, turning to look at her.

'Look at the road, stupid. And drive a little faster please, lover boy, we're late.'

'You seem eager for your fifteen minutes with Rana. You're weird.' She didn't answer. 'And so is he.' I drew up next to a fuming Loquacious. 'I don't know why you hang out so much with him.'

'Someone's jealous,' she said in a singsong voice.

'Of course, I'm burning,' Loquacious shouted as he slipped into the back seat with his shoulder bag. 'Where were you guys?'

I let Pause calm him down, while I turned my thoughts to our nemesis for the night – Rana Vidroh Bahadur Singh. I shivered. By now we'd reached the national highway, and I reacted to the fear by slowing down to sixty on a wide open road. Loquacious put a hand on my shoulder from the back seat, indicating, I presumed, that I should drive faster.

'What do you want?' I snapped, irritated at his attempt at backseat driving.

'Do you want some of this?' He held out a bottle of brandy he had produced from his carry bag. Now we were in business. Courage flowed back into us sip by sip. Brandy bravado. Soon we were conversing animatedly about our first big outstation trip together in high spirits. We even sang old Hindi film songs with Pause in fine form. Unfortunately, as we got closer to the Surajpur canal, the effects of the brandy began to wear off prematurely. Further sips couldn't overpower the trepidation anymore and the talk inevitably veered to the meeting with Rana.

'How should we approach it?' I asked.

Pause didn't want to discuss it too much. 'Plan ahead and you are never flexible in the moment.'

'At least we should decide what we want from our interaction with Rana. Why are we going to his place?' I persisted.

'To free Don, of course.'

'As easy as that! How'll we do it? We need to have a strategy on how to conduct the evening,' I countered.

Loquacious laughed, 'Don't fool yourself. You can't conduct an evening with Rana. From what I understand, he's the one who's in charge.'

'Ah, but don't overlook Don's role in this whole affair...' said Pause. 'And, Sancho, that's two loose cannons too many for me to be able to plan the war. Let's get Don to do the talking and we'll take our chances. '

'He is our best bet in the negotiations,' I agreed, absolving myself of any responsibility.

'All I want to do is negotiate those guns safely...' Loquacious blurted out in an edgy voice. I shook my head in disgust. Sometimes he behaved like an addict seeking his fix of mothering.

'Then you better keep your heroics to a minimum,' I laughed. Realizing I was being cruel by mocking his fears, especially when I was shaking inside myself, I added, 'Don't worry, the MD's got a lot of pressure put on Rana through his political bosses. Nothing will happen. I'm sure those guns will be silent tonight.' I avoided his eyes in the rear-view mirror, so he wouldn't see the doubt in mine.

By the time we came to the massive gate of Rana Vidroh Bahadur Singh's farmhouse, we had all fallen silent. My excuse was the concentration needed to negotiate the slushy road from the Surajpur canal turnoff, probably the result of the downpour earlier. I parked the car beside the Union President's bike. He had met us at the turn to guide us to Rana's farmhouse. Seeing the grave look on the big Sikh's face, dread swarmed down like a hoard of locusts and devoured every kernel of bravado in me. Loquacious too seemed overrun; he sat motionless in the back seat, staring at the gate.

'I want to go home,' I whispered to myself, feeling uselessly in my pocket for my kerchief.

'Same here,' Loquacious whispered back.

If it weren't for Pause, we would never have got out

of the car. She came around to Loquacious's window. Her voice cut through the silence. 'Hello! Asleep, or Sancho's trembling keeping you awake?'

I came to Loquacious's rescue, identifying completely with his fear, 'What's it with you women? It's foolish not to know the meaning of fear. Or are you in denial?'

'No, it's just that you men are too wise. You keep stabbing yourself with all your knowledge of Rana's reputation! You are a petrified thesaurus full of the different synonyms for fear. We women are *otherwise*. We say, why die a thousand deaths when you can only be killed once?'

'What do you suggest we do?' Loquacious came back to life.

'We have a meeting we are late for,' she said, moving determinedly towards the gate.

Reluctantly, the two of us followed her. We left the Union President skulking behind the car. Suddenly he hissed loudly. I looked back at him.

The big Sikh had one stubby finger up. '*Ik ghainta* only, okay? *Tussi* not come *assi* goodbye.' He saluted me. 'Goodbye farmhouse, hello highway.'

I nodded, turned and walked up to Pause who had reached the main gate. Surprisingly there was no guard at the gate. When I mentioned it, Loquacious said, 'Rana's reputation is enough security.'

A jeep stood in the long driveway: a brand new cream-coloured Scorpio. I peered inside out of curiosity and wasn't too surprised to see a rifle sleeping like a baby in the back seat. I looked away immediately, horrified by my own simile. A single lamp lit the driveway. It illuminated a small portion of the massive red brick building as the house rolled on and on in the moonlight.

Pause startled me by smashing the large knocker against the door.

A burst of profanity assailed us. Someone slid back a bolt and swung the tall door open. I gripped my portfolio and readied myself for The Gruesome Giant. To my surprise there was no one there. A loud voice spoke from somewhere near my left knee; I looked down at a dirty dwarf with a long beard.

The hairy dwarf, his rifle taller than him, barked at us. 'What do you arseholes want?'

None of us answered. Loquacious was cowering at the back, tongue-tied, and Pause stood quietly defiant in the face of the profanity because she had earlier requested I do the talking for the group. I gulped down my fright, clenched my fists and, putting on my gruffest voice, said in Hindi, 'We're here to meet Singh Saheb.'

'I'm Mr Singh,' he replied in Hindi too.

'Rana Vidroh Bahadur Singh?' I asked incredulously.

'I'm Veer Vikram Singh. You want Rana Saheb?'

'We have an appointment.'

'Appointment? You're from that gas company,

aren't you? One of your farts is already enjoying our hospitality. Haven't come to take him away, have you? He's so funny. My size too. Can't he move in here for good?' He took a step onto the porch now. 'Ah, let me look at this laundiya! Comely! No problem, you take the old fart. I'll trade him for her.'

I straightened up to my full height. 'Can you please take us to Mr Singh?'

'I have to search you for arms,' the dwarf said without taking his eyes off Pause.

'Look, we have no arms,' I said lifting my arms in the air.

He gave me a murderous look. 'I *have* to frisk. Rana's orders!'

Loquacious mustered up the courage to defend his lady love. Must have been something to do with the size of our opponent. 'If you have to frisk her you get a lady to do it. Isn't there a lady in the house?'

The dwarf gave a lewd smile, a perfect set of teeth shone in his hairy face. 'I wish!' He passed a swollen red tongue over the teeth and gazed at Pause with naked lust. Then, without a warning, the dwarf lunged at Loquacious's balls; the latter jumped backwards off the porch with alacrity and landed on his seat. The dwarf doubled up laughing, clutching his beard for support. When he straightened he said, 'Careful, makkhi! Respect for your seniors! Laundiya, come here, I am not going to hurt you.'

'Frisk your own sister, mister,' Pause told him sternly, stepping back from him.

He burst into laughter again but thankfully that was the last we heard of the frisking. He gestured to us to follow him down a long corridor.

Somewhere along that corridor, I overcame my fear and became conscious of my surroundings. The first thing I registered were the giant paintings. I looked closer and saw they were all canvases of Rana in different poses and regalia, done in the gaudy, larger-than-life style of Bollywood film posters.

So engrossed was I in Rana's art collection, I didn't notice the dwarf stop abruptly at a door to our right. I pulled up hurriedly, avoiding an accident, though my swinging portfolio hit him, causing him to glare at me. We followed him into a room the size of a football field. He announced loudly to no one, 'Visitors, master.'

Suddenly, a voice boomed in Hindi, 'Stepney! Who is it?' I looked around, surprised, for the voice seemed to have come from somewhere close but there was no one around. I expanded my search to the horizon and that's when I saw him. He was a speck in the distance, sitting on a giant throne like a king in his durbar. There were two other people sitting in massive chairs perpendicularly aligned to his throne, so they would have to turn their heads when they spoke to him.

Vir Vikram Singh, a.k.a. Stepney, announced grandly,

'More farts from the gas company, master. There's a laundiya with them who wouldn't let me frisk her.'

'Feeling frisky, Stepney? First lady in our house in years and this is how you treat her?'

Stepney gulped and quickly backed out of the room without another word.

'Come here, you, let me see you better.' Even from across the vast room you could hear him as if he was merely at an arm's length. The room was filled with garlanded photographs of politicians across the colour spectrum from red to saffron. The net had confirmed what I had read in his file: his own politics were difficult to place. He had always maintained that politics was colour-blind.

Unfortunately, his chameleon career hadn't quite lived up to its promise, owing mainly to the sex scandals which had erupted at regular intervals. Even though nothing was ever conclusively proven against him, it was widely accepted that his libidinal overdrive had done his political career in. The teachers' 'jobs for sex' scandal had been the cherry on the cake, earning him the sobriquet of 'Rasputin of Uttar Pradesh'.

We goose-stepped forward in slow motion, admonished at each step with 'Come closer I won't hurt you' till I could smell the cardamom on his breath. Rana sat cross-legged in a dhoti, his massive torso clad in a silk kurta, ramrod straight, head held proudly at an angle that may have been necessitated by his weak eyes. The hair on his head was black and obviously dyed, but his moustache was almost fully white. It twirled into perfect circles on either side of his phallic nose like a pair of testicles.

He glared at us with the intensity of a laser pointer. I found I couldn't move, as if his gaze had reduced us to statues. His eyes may be weak but when he had you within range, boy, could he turn it on.

'Babies! They've sent me babies,' he suddenly thundered. 'Stepney, you paedophile, you want to finger your granddaughter. Bloody cradle-snatcher!' He rumbled on, not having seen Stepney slip away.

Suddenly he laughed, his rage gone as quickly as it had built up. 'Come, kiddies... come to grandpa. Have you come to take your uncle away?'

Released from his gaze by the change in his mood, I decided it was time for the match to begin and reluctantly stepped up to the wicket. 'Rana Vidroh Bahadur Singh, we are here on behalf of every manager and every worker of Frozen Air,' I opened the dialogue cautiously.

'A pimp, boys!' he declared. 'Have you come here to get your wards fucked by me?' His face became dark and he said in a sinister tone, 'By the constitution, I am the MLA of this area; so rightfully they are my constituency and I, Rana Vidroh Bahadur Singh, represent every man and woman in your factory. Right, boys?' He was sharp. You couldn't play mumble with him; he'd steal your leg. I realized

I didn't have the right answers for Rana's ferocious deliveries.

I looked at the two 'boys' on either side of him, whose spanking new rifles defined their personalities. One of them, with a heavily pockmarked face, had a revolver tucked into the waistband of his jeans. I recognized it as Don's revolver, from the distinctly carved hilt. The other one had a boyish face with a deep slash adorning his throat like a choker; apart from his rifle, he sported a knife in a scabbard slung across his chest.

Seeing me beaten, Pause came on to bat valiantly, too valiantly in my opinion. Her naivety at this game came through in the first delivery she faced. 'Look here, sir, you may be the political representative of the area but the Frozen Air staff are our family. The company is like our home. When it burns we will all try to douse out the flames together. You are an outsider with no ownership of Frozen Air. You'll walk away from the burning house when the going gets really tough, as you have from countless others.'

Ouch! She was worse at this than I was. She would lose her wicket in a jiffy. This was no way to bat against Rana. You'd get nowhere trying to hit him out of the ground from the very first ball you faced. You needed to treat him with a lot more respect. Neither Pause nor I had any experience in Industrial Relations (actually the drama tonight was way beyond the strict definition of the term). I felt a more imaginative approach was needed to conduct this business.

Instinctively, I turned to Don Quixote.

Before Rana could reply to Pause I quickly said, 'Let's continue our talks in the presence of our HR Director. It will be more fruitful for you as well, Rana Saheb, to have him in on the dialogue.'

'Yes, it will. I refuse to listen to this laundiya, who is young enough to be my granddaughter, trying to teach me home science. I take a senior manager and all the company can muster up are three kids young enough to be my grandchildren!' He harrumphed. Then he unfolded his legs and stood up. Immediately the two boys, wearing crumpled cotton pyjama-kurtas, jumped up and stood on either side of him; he clasped their shoulders and stepped forward hesitantly. Without the boys, he could barely stand. My dread of him was tinged with pity now, of the sort I sometimes felt for Don. Alpha men who didn't age gracefully were quite nauseating but they did deserve our sympathy. It *was* a deprivation of sorts.

The entourage limped off in the direction of the wall to Rana's left. We reached a small door in the wall made of thick teak, bolted and padlocked from the outside. One of them, the one with the pockmarks, opened the huge lock and hung it in the loop, with the key still inside it. Rana turned and motioned for me to go in first. I had to bend so as not to knock my head against the frame. The size of the door befitted the small room we'd entered, probably a store. It had no windows and an air conditioner on the opposite wall seemed to be the only way to bring in fresh air from the outside. A small door near the AC presumably led to a bathroom. One wall and ceiling was all mirrors, filling the place with multiple reflections. The room had obviously been styled as a love nest. A giant bed complete with purple satin sheets occupied most of the room.

On it lounged Don, oblivious to the freezing temperature or to our entry, despite the noise of the padlock and bolt. He seemed to be in a daydream, staring at himself in the mirrored ceiling. I caught his eye in the reflection and he recognized me at once. 'Oye, Sanchit. Come, I was just thinking about you, boss.' If he was surprised at my presence in his cell, he didn't show it. 'You know that VRS you made didn't go down too well…' He broke off as he saw the others who'd followed me into the room. Pleased to see Rana, he shouted a greeting in Hindi, 'Nana! Welcome to my humble abode!'

Rana winced. 'Nana? *Abey*, I'm younger than you; you just look small! Phhhnnt…' Rana trumpeted through his nose, his moustache clinging to the base of his nostrils like two leaves in a fierce wind. It turned out this was his version of a sigh. He waved a resigned hand at Don; then hobbled up to the head of the bed and patted him on the shoulder, indicating he wanted Don to move from his seat. Don got up dutifully, letting Rana settle down in his place.

Rana said, 'Well, I like this man; he forgives and forgets. The whole district is talking about his humiliation yesterday but he is so happy to see me.' He reached across and slapped Don's tush, and got a smile in return.

'So what brings you here, Nana?' Don asked, sitting on the bed at Rana's feet.

'Ask that question of your young friends here,' he muttered.

'Ah, Pause and Lokesh are here too. I was looking for you, Lokesh. See me when this is over.' Then, playing host, he motioned for all of us to sit down. The boys chose to stand near the door, rifles at the ready. 'Now, tell me, what can I do for you?' He looked politely at Rana.

'For starters let's get it clear once and for all. Do you want to talk to me about the VRS or not? Yesterday you said no, I will not let you come into the plant. Now, this *laundiya* here was telling me... me, Rana Vidroh Bahadur Singh... that your company, what's its name, is like a home and the family who lives in it can deal with its own affairs and I should leave you alone.'

'Why, why, why?' Don sounded alarmed at her words. 'Everybody is welcome. It's party time! Our home is open for all. The more the badmashes the merrier it gets. Whoever wants to talk can come to the party.'

Clearly pleased by Don's line of thinking, Rana declared, 'This is the way to deal with men of my stature.' His moustache was splayed wide with pride, like a peacock's tail. He looked in the general direction of Pause. 'I don't think you understand, woman.'

'We will talk to anybody, Nana, but not to an outsider inside the factory. The factory is for our staff only. So this... this bedroom is a good place for a meeting. Let's start with your basic proposition. What is your demand, Nana?'

'First, pipsqueak, you tell me why you conspired to overthrow the Director General, what's his name?' Rana demanded.

'He had to go! But I don't claim credit for the coup. Some say he's your friend.' Don looked slyly at Rana.

'So you didn't mastermind his ouster. Have I overestimated you? '

'Enough about me, Nana. Let's talk about you. Tell me what's your proposition in all this. What do you want?'

'Negotiate the VRS with me and compensate me for all the trouble I have gone to.'

'I understand the trouble you've taken to bestow your attention on us, and you will be compensated for that, boss, but you must understand a few facts about Frozen Air. You see Aatushi's father took over a family business of textiles way back in the seventies. By the early eighties, he shrewdly decided to diversify into the gas industry and left his uncles to run the textiles business. Mind you, those days textiles were supposed to be the future of India and hardly anybody knew anything about refrigerant gases. But our MD read in some magazine that they were phasing the gases out of Europe. He went and visited a plant in Germany and bought the whole thing there and then. Lock, stock and barrel.'

'Bas! Enough of your small-time seth's story,' Rana barked at him.

'No, no, you don't understand. He is a great visionary. Specially considering how things turned out for the textile industry... and look what's happening to the refrigerant gas industry. We have become the gatekeepers to the ozone hole. We have the keys to close it. We have the world kneeling before us. How visionary is that? But it wasn't only a vision that took Frozen Air to such heights...' I saw Rana's eyes glaze over as Don launched into a long-winded history of the early days of Frozen Air.

After a false start, now we seemed to be on a better wicket. Hopefully Don would prove us right in reposing our trust in him to face all of Rana's overs.

Don seemed to know exactly what to do. He coolly ducked the bouncers, bent away from the beamers, and left the balls falling even a wee bit outside the stumps alone. Anything he couldn't get out of the way of, he defended staunchly with the bat, failing which he got his pads or body in front of his wickets. He never bothered to score a single run off Rana, just kept him at bay, somehow keeping the ball away from his wickets. It didn't look pretty but it was effective. And all the while he kept jabbering at Rana when he came to pick the ball up in his follow-through.

It was this last tactic, the pointless prattling, that ultimately wore Rana down. It was like a missile being asked to smell the roses on the way to its target. After about three quarters of an hour, you could see Don was getting to him. He didn't have many more balls left in him. It was slow, methodical batting, and I began to entertain the hope that with a bit of luck Don would see us through.

He almost pulled it off; if Rana had had to bowl just one more frustrating over, I believe he would have taken himself off the attack. Unfortunately, Mr President at the non-striker's end got himself run out just then.

The door banged open and the President stumbled in! Goading him from behind was Stepney the dwarf. Such was the unexpectedness of their entry that his colleagues at the door missed the President and got Stepney instead. They jumped him from the back, bundling him on to the bed at Rana's feet. Rana barked, 'Can't you see, you blind bastards? Leave him alone, it's Stepney! But who's this ball of hair you've brought with you, Stepney?'

Stepney sat up on the bed, scowling at the 'boys'. 'Master, you know that before sleeping I always brush my teeth at the main gate. I discovered this arsehole there cowering in the lane behind their car.'

Rana recognized the President suddenly. 'Ah… it's Sardarji. What are you doing here?' He boomed.

'I recovered this from him.' Stepney held up a thick steel needle used by Sikhs to stuff errant hair back into the turban. 'It was hidden in his turban.'

Rana's voice filled every nook, cranny, every crevice of the small room, as he screamed, 'WHAT? YOU BABIES WANT TO PLAY ROUGH! You wanted him to storm my fortress and kill me!' You could only marvel at the effect Don had had on Rana, for the latter to think the shivering Union President, armed only with a steel needle the size of a largish toothpick, would be capable of accomplishing such a mission. All of us, even Don, were stunned into silence by Rana's wrath.

'TELL ME, you lamp post, you wanted him to jump me while you pretended to talk…' Rana looked at me when he said this. Stepney let off some of the choicest abuse to underline his master's question. Rana gave him a dirty look and said, 'When I'm speaking you shut up, pipsqueak! And YOU, Sardarji,' he roared. 'You are a local from Surajpur. How dare you BETRAY me?'

The President blubbered incoherently, '*Assi...
tussi... assi...*'

Rana fixed him with a fierce look. '*Assi, tussi, nabbay,
sau, chor nikal kar bhaga.* You are the chor, you have sold
your soul to these outsiders! Sardarji, one thing I can't
stand is disloyalty. It's the end of the road for you.'
Rana glanced at the boy with pockmarks on his face,
obviously his favourite.

'Please, Ranaji,' the Union President sounded
pathetic but I guess the situation demanded he try
everything possible. 'I have a little...' he gulped down
the rest of his words at the sound of the safety catch
of a revolver being pulled back. We all heard it. The
boy held the revolver against the President's temple.

I saw Loquacious close his eyes. Was he going to
faint?

The expression on the President's face was even
more wretched. It reminded me of the last drop
clinging to a tap that has run dry. He had accepted
his fate and was ready to fall.

I felt a pang of guilt. I was somehow responsible
for bringing ruin upon this man. Maybe I shouldn't
have insisted he stay behind waiting for us. I had to do
something to save him. An innocent man was going
to die because of my interference. Ironically, my brief
from the Lazuli Playshop had been to save a life!

Rana gave his final order almost apologetically, as
if it was our fault we hadn't left him with any other
option. 'What are you waiting for? Kill him. Then the

lamp post. Cut both of them into small pieces, stuff them in that bag of his and parcel it to the factory.'

My bag! I remembered the spray can in my portfolio, the one that was supposed to save a life! Sadly, I wouldn't have the time. I watched entranced as Pockmark's forefinger started to press the trigger backwards. Death was about to leap forward and embrace the big Sikh in a bear hug.

'Hey, Pockmarks, why don't you use your own gun?' Don said it quietly, as if the boy was about to use his toothbrush. 'Don't kill him with my gun, Nana, please tell him you can't use somebody else's gun to kill a man… it's very personal.'The boy looked at Rana, confused. Before Rana could issue further orders, Don continued in a very matter-of-fact tone, 'Please ask him to return my gun.'

'Sure, you can have it!' Rana muttered, furiously grinding his teeth. His moustache was splayed like the tail of a cat that had received an electric shock. 'But let's start with the bullets first. Fill the gap in this prattling parrot's upper storey with his own bullets. Shoot him first!'

The boy moved his gun hesitantly from the Union President's forehead, looking askance at his master's confusing orders. He'd been asked to kill three people in the last three minutes. He loved shooting sprees but was now baffled about the order in which he was to kill the men. And he did want to get it right, else he'd be in the doghouse.

He got Don in his sights and looked over at Rana to confirm he'd got it right. The diversion gave me enough time and cover to surreptitiously slide the metal canister out from my portfolio. I fervently hoped the anonymous-looking deodorant spray would deliver what it promised. What could it contain? Mace? Tear gas? I heard Don's plaintive voice, 'No, please! I don't want to die a bachelor…' It was time to go to war.

The first blast went straight up the nostril of the pockmarked boy holding the gun who was more shocked at my action than at the effect of the spray. He arched back from me with a jerk and the hand with the gun jumped protectively up to his nose, cracking it a nasty blow. He released the gun with a loud curse and clutched his bleeding nose with both his hands. With my left hand I picked up the gun from the bed, spraying with all my might in the direction of Rana and Choker. Stepney tried to retrieve his rifle, wrested from him by the other boy, but was a whiff too late.

I shoved the revolver into my shirt and pinched my nostrils shut, glancing over at Pause and Loquacious, who followed my lead. Then I jumped onto the bed and began to pump the atomizer all around like I was being attacked by a swarm of mosquitoes. Everybody was looking at me incredulously. I can only guess at what they must have been thinking because they were all (even Rana) too shocked to speak. The deodorant wasn't particularly strong. It had a slightly sweet odour, which seemed to have no obvious effect on anybody. I looked around foolishly when I had finished the can. By now their surprise had turned to amusement all around but the gas had had no effect. I threw the atomizer disgustedly at the wall, smashing a mirror in the process.

Rana laughed. I cursed the Grand Vizier. I noticed there was a hoarse sound trapped inside Rana's laugh, as if the lion had a bad throat. I was about to let go of my nose, when Stepney began to giggle. Rana looked at him. All Stepney could say was, 'C...c... can't help it... Tee hee hee...' I would have expected Rana to fix him, instead he seemed infected by the same helplessness; he was trying to hold something back and failing miserably. Then the dam broke and the room was flooded with wave upon wave of his laughter. The can had contained laughing gas!

Don snorted and went off into peals, followed by the two boys, and I considered them neutralized as I saw him slide along the mirror onto the floor.

I motioned our team – my friends, the Union President and Don – into the loo. All except Don complied. He was hooting away silently, covering his curtain-like moustache with his lower lip. The gas hadn't affected the three of us yet because with our nostrils shut we hadn't inhaled too much of it. The President would need several more whiffs to erase the sombre mood brought on by his traumatic near-death experience. As we crowded into the bathroom,

Pause wet a towel and, with Loquacious's help, tore it into four strips, which we tied around our noses like masks.

I led the group as we filed out into the small room again. I asked the Union President to gather all the rifles. Don's gun was already with me. I instructed Loquacious to carry Don out with him. Rana was slumped against the bedstead, bulging eyes nearly popping out of his head, tears streaming down from them, mingling freely with the sweat trickling from his hair, and if he hadn't been quietly giggling away into his chest he could have passed off as a man dying of a heart attack. His moustache drooping on one side and upright on the other added to the comic effect. But Pause was far from amused. She went up to Rana Vidroh Bahadur Singh and looked at him with a viciousness I didn't know resided in her. She took a deep breath, as if drawing up all her strength before slapping him. I drew her away.

'Laughing gas, nitrous oxide is also an anaesthetic,' I mumbled through the towel. 'Don't waste your slap, he won't feel it.'

I pushed her out of the room quickly and looked around at the fearsome foursome. They were in various states of mirth. 'You needed that, guys. Loosen up a bit, enjoy yourselves! With compliments from Frozen Air.' I figured, in this closed room, considering the amount of gas I had pumped in, they would remain immobilized for at least an hour.

I yanked out the air conditioner plug from its socket to ensure the fumes remained in the room. Finally, I shut them in with their own lock and key.

'Did you get the joke? What was so funny?' I asked the others who had crowded outside the door. The HR Director was giggling silently into his chest. 'Hope he didn't get too much gas into his head,' I said.

Pause smiled, 'That's all he has in his brain, the gasbag. He's like a hot air balloon. What a ride he took Rana on. He exceeded all my expectations. Thank God we've got him out. He's a crucial part of our plans for tomorrow.'

We all hugged each other in a scene reminiscent to me of the last stage at Lazuli, all except Don who stood tittering on the side. Pause said, 'Sancho Panza to the rescue! You saved Don Quixote again!'

I looked at Don and said, 'The question is, how do you save him from himself?' As an afterthought I added, 'Actually, you know what I suspect, it's all an act. He isn't as foolish as he makes himself out to be. Anyway, let's get going. Loquacious, I suggest you take him and the Union President on the bike to the company guesthouse at the plant. Pause and I have some unfinished business to complete and I'll join you afterwards.'

Both of them looked at me, puzzled. I put a hand on his shoulder. 'Someone needs to prop him up on the bike. And remember in his letter he asked you to "find me wherever I am". When the effect of the gas wears off you can ask him what he meant.'

CHAPTER 8

The Revelation

My outstanding performances on Pause's terrace and in Rana's love nest within a couple of hours had boosted my confidence like never before in this corporate game. It was like scoring a century in each innings of a test match. And the selectors had been watching in a manner of speaking. When I reported my feats back to the Grand Vizier I would be admitted to the portals of a Dream Team of the corporate world, a team that admitted only the crème de la crème of crusaders out to revolutionize the game.

You can't blame me for brimming with self-belief for the first time in a decade. And so I wasn't surprised by the slight swagger with which I invited Pause to sit on Rana's throne when we were alone.

'Yes, this is a fitting set for the finale,' I said as if talking to myself but loud enough for her to hear. I took off the towel from my face and wiped Don's revolver with it methodically. I walked over deliberately to one of the large velvet-covered chairs on her left and regally lowered myself into it.

'What is it, Sancho? Before Lokesh left you told him you and I had some unfinished business. Hope you don't mean what we started on my terrace? I am not in the mood...'

I turned my head slowly to the right and looking into her eyes, I said, 'Pause, I have a feeling you already know what I'm going to say. So let's not fool each other anymore.' Indira Gandhi was smiling in a portrait directly behind her. Probably the shrewdest prime minister we'd had. And certainly the most controversial. It was fitting that Pause was sitting below her. She, too, was a sovereign with pernicious designs. At least Indira had attempted her 'reforms' openly without cowering behind a screen of anonymity.

She looked at me confused by my sudden change in character. 'You're scaring me, Sancho. What is it?'

'Okay. Since you refuse to take off your mask, let me do the honours.' With all the grandness I could muster, I bowed down low and said, 'Master Craftsman of The Progress in Work Collective, Pause Daniels, I pay tribute to your ambition and to a vision for a just and equal society.'

She stared at me with unmoving eyes, not at all surprised by my lifting the veil off her secret world. A

peel of booming laughter from the room behind me
further killed the drama I had tried to build up.

'I know who you are, Pause. You can drop the
pretence.'

'And I know who *you* are, Sanchit Mishra,' came
her repartee in a steely voice that ran through my soul
like a sword. 'Keeper of The Shareholders' Conscience,
why must you talk through the barrel of a gun?'

'How the fuck...' I exclaimed, lowering Don's
revolver onto my lap.

'...did I come to know about you?' She finished
the sentence for me. 'You tell me all and I will do the
same. But you start.'

I clutched Don's revolver tighter through the towel
wrapped around my palm, pointing it in her general
direction. 'Why should I start?'

'You made the first move, lover boy.'

'All right.' Amidst raucous laughter from inside the
locked room, I admitted to my deal with the devil. 'I
am in touch with The Shareholders' Conscience. But
I'm not a Keeper, whatever that means.'

'How did they get to you?' she asked. I could feel
her eyes boring through me.

How *had* it happened? How had things reached
such a pass? It had all started so innocuously. I
thought back to my first contact with them.

'Someone called the Professor is all I know of The
Shareholders' Conscience. For a long time I didn't
even know what the outfit was called. I assumed

this Professor was a freelance investor like Soros or Buffet.'

'Where did you meet the Professor?'

'Three years back, you remember I had gone to Dubai for a salary survey for the new plant? You were there too, as a part of the team who'd gone scouting for the location. I was handed a slip in my apartment one evening – it was an invitation to a friendly chat; there was an address of a chat room and the identity I was to assume in it. The first interaction was a tame affair and all we did was to agree to get in touch in the same chat room at an appointed time every full moon night, a practice we have followed ever since, though we've changed chat rooms several times. I began by passing on information for which a small sum was deposited in a bank account in my name. Back then I didn't know the Professor had anything to do with The Shareholders' Conscience. In fact, he never mentioned The Shareholders' Conscience until a month ago.'

'What kind of information was he looking for?'

'Oh well, it was all from Godfather's office. Secrets about the cartel, you know, minutes from their monthly parleys where they planned the price and production quotas, stuff like that. Also, the details of the whole carbon trading mechanism that Godfather set up. And how the money was distributed among his people. He had accounts for every single paisa, you could fault him for everything else but there was no hanky-panky in the monies.'

'How did you get all this information?'

'My mole was Ram Jag, the peon posted in Godfather's office.'

'Ah! Thank God. I thought you'd managed to corrupt Lokesh.'

'Loquacious? Ha! You think Godfather would trust that leaking bucket? In any case the Professor hinted that he didn't want Loquacious involved.'

'How did the Professor catch on to me?'

'I don't know. I knew nothing about The Collective or The Shareholders' Conscience till full-moon night a month ago, when the Professor made me a party to all this intrigue.' Like the proverbial frog in the pot I hadn't realized the water was heating up. By the time it had started to boil it was too late to jump out. 'It was in that chat that he told me about you being the Master Craftsman of The Collective and he ordered me to do this.'

'To do what? What exactly are your orders?'

'Kill you.' As I uttered those words a sense of urgency gripped me. The room behind me was eerily silent. Maybe the effect of the gas was beginning to wear off. 'Then a fortnight ago an invitation from The Collective landed up at my desk. I knew it was you who had nominated me but I couldn't figure out why. In the beginning I thought Turkey would be a good chance to unmask you and finish off my assignment. Then I did some research about this Collective of yours and realized that I quite agreed with their noble agenda; suddenly I was in two minds. I reached the underground city, still undecided. The location was perfect but of course you had given me the slip.'

'What's wrong with this place? This is an ideal spot to complete your assignment, Sancho. You can blame it on Rana.'

I gulped down a ball of fear and sat up in my chair, letting the revolver drop in my lap again.

'Go ahead then.'

I said with a sigh, 'I can't do it.'

'How much are they paying you?'

'It was never about the money.'

'Why did you agree to do it then?'

'I'm sick of this corporate game. I've struggled in poor form for years now. I want out. The Professor promised me a high position in the Board of Cricket Control, India.' I don't know why I felt the need to explain all this to her.

'So, what's the problem now? Finish your assignment and get your reward, Sancho.'

'I can't. When I took on the assignment I didn't expect to fall in love with you.'

There was sporadic banging on the door. Had I grossly overestimated the concentration of the nitrous oxide in the can? It had saved a life and that's all it was meant for. But we couldn't leave yet, not until I had cleared things up somewhat.

'I am holding the gun and you're doing all the interrogation. You tell me all about The Collective. When did you join them?'

'A month ago.'

'What? Just a month ago? Then how come...'

'How come I became The Master Craftsman?' She completed my question. Then answered it too. 'Well, I appointed myself.'

'What are you saying?'

'There is no Collective, Sancho.'

'What do you mean? Lazuli wasn't a figment of my imagination?'

'Not yours but mine. I made the whole thing up. They were all hired actors. I was there too. One of the five.'

'No way! You're putting me on.'

'A few days of practice, mate, is all.'

My God, she sounded just like the Brit.

'If you wanted a hug you should have told me.' If I closed my eyes I could have sworn the Brit was sitting in front of me. 'Some acting, eh?' She smiled.

'And...' I cupped my hands in front of my chest.

'Bit of padding...' Noticing me narrow my disbelieving eyes, she added, 'Okay, a huge amount of padding.'

'What about the postcard? The Journal? The website? The Quiver?' I rattled off all the signposts of the alternative world that had swallowed me in. 'All a hoax?'

'The postcard as you know was typed and delivered by me. And issues of The Journal in the library are just shells. Only labels on box files, there's nothing inside them. The websites I set up last month. The Quiver, or The Charter as I called it, is genuine stuff, though. Articles from my own experience and research.'

A loud banging started from inside the room. Or was it inside my head? All the loose ends were knocking about in my cranium. 'So, if The Collective is all a hoax, then The Shareholders' Conscience too doesn't exist! Oh my God!'

'I'll explain it all on the way. We'd better get out of here fast.'

Somebody was trying to kick the door down amidst loud yelling from inside. Reluctantly I had to agree to terminate the conversation for now.

The raucous caucus had almost broken through the door by the time we left the farmhouse. As I switched on the ignition, I heard the door give way with a splintered crash.

Once we were on our way, I took it easy; there didn't seem any need to make a scorching getaway. I calculated Rana wouldn't bother chasing us, thinking we were far away by now.

Of course we knew it wasn't the last we had seen of him. He would certainly come after us again. Our Great Escape would make him the laughing-stock of the region if he didn't take revenge soon. And, on his second try, I was sure it would be his guns that would do most of the talking.

Even so it wasn't Rana or his next attempt we spoke of on our journey back. In fact, till we hit the main road, Pause and I didn't talk at all. I concentrated on the gushing flow of water in the Surajpur canal glinting in the moonlight, while trying to keep my mind off the watershed that had risen between us.

On reaching the turn off I slipped the car on to the main road towards Surajpur and the factory guest house where we were to stay the night. At this late hour, the national highway was almost deserted; a few trucks whizzed by like planets lost in their own world. I wondered if Pause and my orbits, too, were about to separate forever.

It was Pause who brought it up first. 'So?' she asked looking straight ahead. 'Where to from here?'

'Plant guest house I suppose,' I said, skirting dangerous ground.

But she seemed determined we negotiate the awkwardness right away. 'What about us, I meant.' I looked out of the window at the endless fields of mustard stretched out on either side of the road under a silver sky; gold in silver light, it seemed pretty dull. I noted the combination didn't exactly get on like a

house on fire as it did in daylight. Did it signify our
fate too? After the revelations could we ever rekindle
the flame that we had lit on the terrace?

'Us?' I asked rhetorically. 'Is there anything left to
talk about? I am supposed to be your assassin. How
will we ever get over that?'

'Simple. I'll just abort the assignment. I can see
your heart's not in it anymore.'

'You? What about the Professor? It's full moon
tonight,' I said, craning my neck to look up through
the windscreen. 'He's going to ask me what
happened.'

She too bent forward gazing at the beautiful orb
high up, a silver bindi adorning the dark brow of the
sky. 'I know. You and the Professor hook up around
midnight to chat and it's almost midnight now. But
tonight let's chat face to face. The car can be our chat
room.'

I looked over at her. 'Now you're claiming you are
the Professor too.' My tone was disbelieving though
I knew she had to be telling the truth. It all made
sense. 'Master Craftsman, Participant at the Playshop,
Professor – how many masks do you wear?'

'As many as it takes to transform you.'

'Transform me? Into a killer? From a petty
information peddler to an assassin is quite a
transformation. Why are you doing this? Why did
you pay me for spying earlier and then try to seduce
me into becoming your killer?'

'It's my turn to come clean, Sancho. The whole truth and nothing but. We owe ourselves a fresh start based on trust. It all began three years back. Aatushi and I came together to restore Frozen Air to its people. Wrest it away from Godfather who was running the place despotically into the ground. He'd taken the company out of Aatushi's father's hands and had no plans of giving it back. He had mounted two hostile takeover bids by proxy. Did you know that? But the family managed to hang on. After his second bid we decided to take the war to his camp. To start our little battle, we needed information from inside his camp. What was he up to? Why was the cartel so important? What were his plans for the future? That's where you came in.'

'Why me?'

'I don't know. I just had a feeling you'd swing it for us with your people engagement skills. Also, I researched your past a bit and the match-fixing scandal seemed to indicate you could be persuaded to join forces with us.'

We drove along silently for a while. I thought I'd left the blasted match-fixing scandal behind. It had been the lowest point in my life. The enquiry had not been able to prove anything but it had taken its time. And its toll on my career. Having been banned from first-class cricket while the enquiry was on (almost eighteen months), my confidence had combusted and my talent had been in tatters. When the committee had declared me eligible for selection again, a few half-hearted innings had produced dismal failures. I tried honestly to revive my dream with practice and focus. But dreams can't be invoked at will. They are born out of a context and no two contexts can ever be the same. There was no going back to square one. I had moved on. Time to lay down the bat and retool myself to play another game. Except it wasn't as easy that. The corporate game had taken its toll; I'd never really been comfortable playing it. And then this: how was I to know the ghost of the scandal would come back to haunt me here?

'I don't know what you see in me…' I wondered aloud. 'I'm ashamed of myself. What do I say? I'm just not worthy of your love…' I looked out of the window and through the blur of my tears I saw the night rushing by in a hurry to reach somewhere.

'Sancho!' Pause suddenly screeched.

I had almost swayed into the path of an oncoming truck whose driver was dipping his headlights maniacally at me. I swerved back to my side of the road but couldn't retain control of the wheel and slid off onto the narrow unpaved track beyond which was a steep ditch about ten feet and two dead bodies deep. We bumped along, one tyre on the road and the other on the unpaved track, for fifty metres or so. There was no way I could swing the car back onto the road. I had to stop it somehow. I jammed the brakes! The car skidded and for a few seconds the left rear wheel was hanging in the air. My next memory is of Pause yelling, 'Gently...' so loud that I had to comply; the most difficult part was the steering but somehow I kept it straight till we came to a dead stop.

I looked across at her nervously, my eyes wide. She began to laugh. 'Wow, that was fun. I didn't know you were a rally driver!' I smiled weakly at her.

She went on, 'Let's do it again! But before that let me kiss you goodbye.' Saying this, she slid over to my side, held my face with both her hands and planted her lips on mine. Eager to get the car back on the road I tried to draw away but she held on to me, prolonging the kiss into a long passionate one. I succumbed and opened my mouth to let her tongue explore my tonsils. When she disengaged her lips, I was panting for air and for more.

Pause said, 'There! Are you feeling more worthy of my love now?' I gulped down a lungful of air in reply.

I got the car back on the road while I thought about her question. Why had she invested so much in a despicable criminal like me without a value system? The only thing I had going for me was I was open to influences. I listened, I let things affect me and my skin wasn't so thick that the world couldn't make an imprint on it. Once in a while, I opened my doors wide and let in the light to cleanse my insides. That was the sum total of my strengths. Pause interrupted my deliberations to hand me a Malabar parota roll

with jam. As I munched into it, I felt the jam ooze
through into my mouth. That bite symbolized my
last month: I had been like a dog nibbling idly at a
bone, when suddenly I had bitten right through to
the marrow of life and now, as the juices filled my
mouth, I wasn't sure what to make of it.

'You know why I played The Collective hoax on
you?' Pause broke through my reverie.

I looked over at her blankly.

She continued, 'I realized you were disillusioned
with the corporate world thanks mainly to Godfather's
bullying ways for the last seven years. The tyrant had
systematically squashed your self-esteem. But I knew
you had potential. Lots of it. I also knew how you
hankered to be in a crack team. I wanted to give you
the feeling that was almost in your grasp many years
ago. I thought the high might pull you out of the
morass you'd sunk into.'

'The Playshop at Lazuli was something else, I agree.
What a fantastic design. I did come back feeling
different. As if my spine had been starched. But
how long could it last? Remember, the assignment
to kill you was running parallel to The Collective's
assignment to "save a life". How much weirder can
it get? Why set it up like that? If the Professor wasn't
playing my evil side, I could have fooled around
with The Collective for a while longer. A few more
assignments with them might have done the trick.'

'This way it was quicker, wasn't it? Play the evil and the good side of you to the hilt. See which wins.'

I stared at her in disbelief. She was still toying with me. Wasn't she? 'And what's the verdict?' I asked cynically.

'You're ready, Sancho. Ready for tomorrow!'

'Tomorrow? What's happening tomorrow?'

'Tomorrow we hand over the ownership of the company to the people. Remember our discussion in the library this morning? After that I convinced Aatushi of her folly in the way she'd implemented the VRS. I gave her an alternate, sustainable way forward and she's agreed to give my idea a try: We're putting up The Frontline Parliament in the plant.'

'What?' The term seemed familiar.

'You don't remember a mention of it from The Charter?'

'The Charter?'

'That folder ...'

'Ah, right. The Quiver. I guessed you'd composed the entire document. Clever stuff, Pause.' I touched my forehead with my fingers in a salute to her handiwork.

'You ain't seen nothing yet.' A sinister smile played on her lips. 'What do you have in store?'

'The Frontline Parliament in *action* tomorrow.'

I stopped the car and pulled over off the highway onto the kerb. I remembered the article in The Quiver on ownership. Though the Frontline Parliament had been mentioned in it, I didn't recall there being an elaborate description of it.

'What are you doing?' Pause asked.

I put on the overhead light in the centre of the car's ceiling. I took The Quiver out of my portfolio. 'Let me quickly refresh myself by reading that article, please. And then you can have your Charter back.'

Owners Sans Ownership

The shareholder paradox

Ten per cent of the US population possesses about 85% stocks and 90% bonds of US corporations. This group of about ten million households thus owns a large swathe of the corporate world. In 2000 it was estimated that the richest 2% owned 51% of global assets.

Own. It's a strong word used loosely to denote possession. Let's delve a little deeper. Can an investor of capital own the company by merely buying its shares?

The difference between owning shares and ownership

We argue that mere possession of shares

doesn't bestow ownership. Ownership is not about capital; it is about labour. Most shareholders will never set foot in the company all their lives. All they want is profitable returns for their investment by any means. The difference between the staff who toil in the firm and the shareholder is akin to that between the farmer and an absentee landlord. Or between a real mother and a surrogate one.

Of the 475 companies that crashed out of the Fortune 500 list in the last fifteen years, our research shows that the decline in 90% of the cases came as a consequence of decisions taken at the behest of the shareholders. We attach 25 real stories compiled by insider core members of The Collective to corroborate our case.

Sure, the shareholder's money helps to buy needed assets; often, entire companies are acquired with the money. But consider this - when I mortgage my house to a bank, it doesn't become theirs; the bank is the moneybags, which helps me to own the place but the ownership remains with me. The same logic applies to a corporate - the shareholders are the moneybags and the employees who nurture the company are its real owners.

The difference between ESOPs and ownership

We believe capital is a mere enabler and buying the shares of the company does not transfer ownership to the possessor of these pieces of paper. Some companies have tried to transfer ownership to employees through ESOPs or Equity Stock Option Plans which were quite in vogue in the early years of this millennium.

But we argue that by giving shares to the employees you don't distribute ownership; instead, you take it away. These employees start to think short-term like the shareholder in terms of maximizing the market capitalization of their stock. Decision-making inside the firm suffers. In any case, real ownership (in the sense we mean it) is always taken, never given.

What do we mean by real ownership?

At the core of the firm's success is the labour performed/ value added to the asset bought with capital. We're not suggesting a Marxian revolution led by the proletariat; rather, a quiet internalization of the reality behind ownership. When you transfer ownership to these real owners and they begin to

work for themselves, not for a set of
unknown shareholders, it will give them
an opportunity to make work meaningful;
it will give them freedom and joy
evident in people allowed to set their
own agendas.

Why is ownership the key?

Most importantly the company where
people take ownership of the common
agenda will flourish like never before.
The staff of an organization needs
the flexibility provided only by real
ownership because at every step they
encounter situations they'd never dreamt
of, let alone planned for. They have to
keep creatively adjusting the shoe to
the emerging path as they walk towards
a shared goal. If they don't have
ownership of their work they are going
to have to come back to the 'owners' at
every single step, asking how to deal
with the simplest of dilemmas. In an
emerging world every action throws up
a unique dilemma; it's impossible to
sort all these out beforehand at the
head office and make manuals for how
to run an organization. One central
engine or owner isn't enough to pull
us all through to the shared goal. We
need millions of engines with their own

dynamos producing energy all the time to transport us to the Promised Land.

In the bargain the shareholders prosper too because such joyful labour creates a successful firm. They can take their share of profits (in proportion to the value they brought in) but let ownership remain in the hearts of the people who run the business. We need to rewire corporate decision-making for this to happen.

In a related article we argue that the share market, our new God, is intrinsically flawed in that the way it's structured it doesn't promote the responsible behaviour needed of an owner.

A tool to create such ownership among the employees called the Frontline Parliament is being smithed on the anvil as of now...

'You write so well. It's inspiring. Though you haven't explained the tool in this.' I tossed the folder on her lap. 'Why do you call it a Parliament?'

'Because the body will take decisions. They won't just exchange ideas, they will fight, they will debate and finally they will arrive at a kind of consensus on how to go forward; something like what's

supposed to happen in a Parliament. The thing is
that ownership, I believe, comes from constructing
something together. When you've put in one of your
bricks into the edifice of a concept as it is being built,
you feel belongingness to the idea. And it comes from
creating a space where Deep Democracy prevails. A
place where your opinion is respected, where the
final decision has been discussed with you, that place
you call your own.'

'I don't think I fully understand.' I negotiated a
roundabout and took the road leading us off the
national highway and into the town of Surajpur.
The streetlights weren't working. The shops were all
closed, some people slept on the pavement while
others were spreadeagled on their thelas. A lone man
stood peeing against a wall on the far side.

'Simply put, it's a space which allows collective
decision-making. Tomorrow Aatushi will unveil it.
I won't steal her thunder by telling you any more
about it now but we need you by our side. Hope I
can count on you.'

'I don't know if I can count on myself, honestly.
I have a kind of fatal flaw. I self-destruct at the last
minute. I am honoured, though, by the attention you
have bestowed upon me and the energy that's gone
into trying to change me. I don't know how I can ever
repay you. Then there is the actual cost involved. This
trick you played on me must have cost you a packet.'

'Aw, it was peanuts.' I frowned at her; it had to be a substantial sum. 'You see, Aatushi gave me a cut from the money she made from the deal with Unified Air. So, I am a rich woman. Very rich.'

We reached the company guest house half an hour before midnight. There were lots of guests from the Head Office, so I had to share a room with Loquacious, who, the sleepy-looking caretaker told me, had reached the guest house almost an hour back. I opened the unlocked door to the roar of a train thundering towards me. On closer inspection, the noise turned out to be Loquacious snoring. He lay on his back, hands folded across his chest, jaw thrust out, breathing through his open mouth so loudly that it felt like a freight train running through my head. It is a marvel how this simplest of tasks performed by billions of us without a fuss becomes so strenuous in the case of a large section of human males.

I could have turned him around gently on his side but it would only get me temporary relief. There was no point in asking apnoea to leave politely; it inevitably returned louder than before.

I would have to be brutal. The only way to escape a tortured night was to throw Loquacious out of the room. 'Hi!' I barked loudly, standing behind his head. He woke with a start and sat up in bed. Seeing nobody around, he jumped out like a scared child, convinced a ghost was about. I came around the bed and stood in front of him. He looked at me blankly until his mind returned from its nocturnal grazing to occupy his head again. I discerned the homecoming by the way his eyes showed recognition of what might have happened. He said lovingly, 'You bastard, why did you wake me up?'

'You were having a respiratory attack!'

'Sancho. Why?' he asked, sternly this time.

'You were breathing loud enough to bring the roof down.' I showed him a piece of plaster I had broken off the wall.

'I can't help myself.' He lay down again and turned away.

'You don't need any more help. I, on the other hand, could do with a lot of it. I've hardly slept for the past three days. And tomorrow promises to be a killer!'

'But I can't stop snoring!'

'No, you can't, but you can drag your mattress out to the living room and snore there.'

'Why?'

'Because I can't sleep on a railway platform. And since it is your freight train making all the noise it's only fair you drive it out to the living room.'

'You are a bastard! Anyway, I'll do it because you saved our lives today, Sancho.'

'By the way, you better get a nose job soon, unless you want to sleep alone all your life.'

'Too late. Even with my handicap, I'm not a virgin like you.'

'I'm sure you've never slept with the same woman twice. Am I correct?'

He paused, not for long. He admitted sheepishly, 'Come to think of it, I haven't. Because of my snoring, you think? Is it that bad?'

'Well, you could always find a station master's daughter who might rubbish my claims, or you could meet a deaf princess. Of course, a simple nose job would open up the field a wee bit more.'

He got up with a sorrowful expression and was quiet while we heaved his mattress out to the living room and dumped it at the far end, near the door to another bedroom. We'd just laid out the mattress and were covering it with a sheet when we heard the unmistakable sound of a superfast express from behind the door. We both looked at each other.

'Don.' Loquacious whispered ruefully. 'He's in that room.' I had to strain to hear what he was saying.

'Why are you whispering?' I shouted over the din. 'Nothing but a head-on collision with your freight train will wake him. What about you? Will you be able to restart your engine?'

'He won't disturb me,' said Loquacious and lay down.

I sat on a chair and asked him, 'Got here without any more adventures?'

He nodded.

'Did Don tell you why he was looking for you?'

'Oh, that! Nothing much really. He told me something I already knew – Pause is a close confidante of the MD's daughter.'

I stuck my not very strong chin into my chest and asked indignantly, 'You knew it?'

'Yes, they shared rooms in college or something.' In another era I would have been intensely jealous of him knowing secrets I hadn't been privy to, but as of this evening I was somewhat less insecure.

'Apparently, it was a recent revelation to Don,' he clarified.

'And why was this news a matter of "life and death"? Weren't those the words he used in the note to you?'

'It was a matter of life and death for him. You see, since the coup, he'd been treating me suspiciously (as a DG loyalist); he'd even got me on a kind of hit list, he said. When he came to know how close Pause and Aatushi were he took me off it because he didn't want Pause to get the impression he was creating trouble for me. He knows how close the two of us are. He thought Pause might tell Aatushi and that would spoil things for him with the new CEO. Anyway, he assured me his suspicions about me are a thing of the past.'

'Pathetic!' I closed the conversation abruptly, having lost interest. I fell silent mulling over the day. Loquacious turned away from me. I don't know how long I sat there. My reverie broke when I said to myself, 'I love you.'

'And I hate you,' Loquacious replied.

Returning to my room, I turned in immediately thinking of the early start the next day, though it took me another hour to conquer my roving mind and fall asleep.

At ten the next day a gate meeting was held just outside the wall of the plant, in which the Union President took the microphone to announce the change in management policy regarding the VRS. Don's presence at this meeting, as requested by Pause, created quite a stir. For one, this was the first time such a senior manager was sharing a platform with the Union President at a gate meeting, though that wasn't the main reason for the crowd's excitement at seeing Don on the stage. Reports of his escape from Rana's custody had been spreading since dawn. Don was well on his way to becoming a part of regional folklore. The report, probably filed by the Union President, gave disproportionate credit to Don for the getaway. Ram Jag, who told me about it at breakfast, spoke of Don wresting his gun back from Rana's henchman and shutting them all in a room before escaping on the President's bike. The crucial part I and the laughing gas had played had been conveniently airbrushed from the account. I guess the President's funny bone wasn't tickled even a wee bit due to his sombre mood.

I remember eking out a lesson from Ram Jag's account of the events of the night before: 'People perceive reality from their own persona. Worse, they react to these thoughts in their heads thinking they are responding to reality.' This had come across so starkly at the Lazuli Playshop.

I didn't bother to correct Ram Jag's version since it was possible that when the report reached Rana he too may go along with the airbrushed story and I might escape his wrath. I saw there were benefits to this anonymity business, too.

So it was an emboldened Union President, riding on his part in Don's getaway, who took on Rana obliquely by adopting the line that Frozen Air should handle its affairs internally. Nobody had dared to declare this in public yet (Pause had done so yesterday but behind closed doors) and the buzz that greeted the President's avowal was proof he'd set the cat among the pigeons.

Don's presence lent immense credibility to the President's claims about the management agreeing to rethink the VRS based on a representation by the union. He said the MD's daughter was to unveil a participative process for review at 4.00 p.m. that day and he urged everybody to be present irrespective of their shifts.

So they were. A balmy day with a cool wind witnessed the largest staff turnout in the history of any event at Frozen Air. We assembled in a parachute tent erected for the meeting in an open ground in front of the canteen. It was the first public speech the new CEO would be making and that in itself was a huge draw; what made the event compelling was the Union President's endorsement of a management rethink on the VRS in his gate meeting earlier in the day. All workers to a man were present. In anticipation of the event, the previous night's shift had been cancelled and all personnel had been called in for the general shift to facilitate their participation. It wasn't just workers, though; people from all levels in the organization were there. And not just from the plant, a large contingent came in from the Head Office as well. The event had been scheduled so that staff from Delhi could drive down in special shuttles commissioned for the occasion. Everybody across the hierarchy was curious to know about the altered composition of the poison that had instilled insecurity and instability into the very core of the organization.

'Welcome to the Frontline Parliament!' Aatushi's unusual greeting grabbed the attention of the audience. She spoke in perfect Hindi. 'This space will be playing an important role in our lives from now on. This is the space where we'll shape our common destinies together, this is the space where we'll take decisions collectively, and this is the space where we'll co-create our future.' She paused. 'But I am getting ahead of myself. The Frontline Parliament actually comes much later. Let me start where Pause Daniels did. Many of you know her – she's the Product Strategy Head and has been with us for nearly fifteen years. It is with her that I'd like to share credit for conceptualizing this space. Pause posed a fundamental question to me the other day: "Who owns this company?"'

The MD was conspicuously absent, presumably sending the message that he had full faith in his daughter's leadership. I was not so sure about Janice Kramer, though, who sat directly behind the lectern against which Aatushi was leaning. The other occupants of the stage were the Union President and Don.

Pause whispered to me, 'Surprising, Janice is here. That too sharing the stage.'

I hadn't expected her either after her emphatic refusal to have any truck with the rewiring of the VRS. Don kept bending towards the grey head of the American and whispering something in her ear, presumably translating the speech into English for her.

You could never have guessed this was Aatushi's first public speech by the way she was working the crowd; she had them hanging on to even her silences.

'I thought about what Pause had asked me. I knew it was a trick question but I couldn't figure out where she was going with it so I gave her the straightforward answer. I said, "My father and I own 25 per cent, the rest is with Unified Air or more precisely with specific shareholders of Unified Air." Pause smiled at my answer and said something to me that changed my paradigm of ownership forever. She turned all that I stood for on its head. She said, "Aatushi, that's exactly the thinking due to which we are in this mess. Sorry, you don't own this company. Neither does your father. Nor do the shareholders of Unified Air, most of whom will never see this plant in their lives. What kind of ownership is that? They've just invested some capital into the company with which we can buy new technology. All they want is profitable returns for their investment." Deep down somewhere I knew Pause was right. What she said started off a deep introspection within me and it's from this reflective space that I open up my heart to you today. I ask you the same question: Are we shareholders the real owners of Frozen Air?'

Her tone had turned personal; she was in a dialogue with each one of us. The sincerity with which she spoke made me realize I had grossly misread this woman. She'd been waiting all her life for the right moment to establish her thrall and this was clearly it.

'Tell me, if you take a loan to build a house does the bank own your house? Of course not! It's yours and you look after it with full responsibility and ownership. Because you live in it! Likewise, we shareholders don't own Frozen Air… This company is yours! You live in it! You've just taken a loan from us shareholders to modernize it. For you, working here does not only mean making money, like it does for the shareholders. Sure, livelihood is important but paramount is making meaning in your lives. Pride, camaraderie, fun and learning – a workplace should provide its staff with all of that because work defines your lives. You spend the best part of your day here. Time is more important than money today. The place should be handed over to those who devote energy and time to it, to run with full ownership rights.'

All this was surely dangerous territory as far as Unified Air was concerned, though the serene Mona Lisa half smile of the short, grey-haired American lady betrayed none of it. Until Don translated Aatushi's latest idea. A storm broke on Mona Lisa's face; her eyebrows flew heavenwards, her eyes dripped molten lava and as she bent over to clarify a point with Don, I saw the large mole under her aquiline nose bob up and down. I had always found her face familiar; now the bobbing mole revealed to me her true identity. She was Professor Janus Gemini, editor of Human Chain, from whose interview on the web I had first heard of The Charter. I bent towards Pause with a puzzled look, 'Isn't she the editor of Human Chain?'

'No, silly. I just used a video of her speaking at a meeting that I happened to have. I needed an American face for Professor Janus Gemini. It was the only one I could get my hands on readily. I didn't think you would be able to tell who it was from the stamp-sized grainy close-up of her talking head. I forgot about the mole, I guess. The voiceover is mine.'

'Oof, you are too much! You really manipulated me!'

'Nothing compared to what that bitch will do, given half a chance. I don't like her one bit. Too feudal. Look how she's losing her shirt over giving up a tiny button of control to the staff. She's going to disrupt this Frontline Parliament, I suspect. We'll have to deal with her somehow.'

I looked at the faces in the crowd; agitation was writ large there too, but for totally different reasons. They were confused at this offer of ownership being extended to them by the new CEO. They would have been happy with the mere removal of the VRS, hanging like Damocles's sword on the main notice board.

Aatushi wasn't planning on giving them (or herself) an easy way out, though. 'I am part owner of Frozen Air from my role as a worker here, not as a shareholder, mind you, and I'm willing to share this ownership with the rest of you. Do you want to take it on? How many of you are interested? Put up your hands if you would like to become collective owners of this company.'

It was a brave way of gauging their reaction. At first everybody looked around to see what effect her words had had on the others. There seemed to be lots of doubt in the air but there were certainly no hands.

It turned out to be a mere matter of initiation, though, and once the Union President had raised both his hands on the dais the whole crowd was 'up in arms'. It was a humbling sight. I'm not sure everybody understood the significance of raising their hands but they nevertheless went ahead and placed their trust in their colleagues who did.

The sea of hands, though, couldn't overwhelm the hierarchies in its swell, as most of the senior managers hesitated to embrace her offer. Why would they want to willingly hand over their decision-making powers? Aatushi quickly jumped into the turbulent waters to reassure the senior management they needn't worry, because they would still play an important facilitative role in the Parliament to ensure informed and democratic decision-making. Freed from operational decision-making, they could rise to the strategic challenges facing Frozen Air. The managers, especially the plant management, were still cynical, I could tell, but there would be time enough to bring them around. It was the workers who had to be won over today and there she'd made considerable inroads.

She encouraged everyone to wear an organization hat along with their own. She urged them to look around, engage with organizational issues, and not bow their heads purely in their own work. On her part she promised to listen to every idea, attend to every protest and respect all contributions.

Finally she came to the contentious issue of the VRS, whose need she explained with a quick recap of the big picture in which she included a simplified 'Montreal Protocol for Dummies'. A big screen behind her detailed the new skills that would be required for the new technologies Unified Air would be bringing in. She emphasized this as the origin of the idea of the VRS. I was amazed at the transparency she displayed in accepting that she herself had had doubts about some of the old guard having the potential to learn these new tricks.

'But then Pause helped me realize we'd condemned the people without asking them if they thought they could make the grade. That's where the Frontline Parliament comes in. Let's use it to co-create a consensus on the way forward. So the question to you, the new owners of Frozen Air is' — it was flashed on the screen — 'Do we need the VRS? Let's construct the answer together in the spirit of Deep Democracy.

Put your thoughts on a brick and add it to the wall at the back.'

People were handed small brick-shaped cards with permanent markers and asked to Agree, or Disagree, or remain Uncertain, giving reasons and suggestions. The card had a sticky substance like a Post-it on the back which would help them attach it to the wall.

The sun was sinking on the main shed which housed the plant as the people got down to the task at hand. The giant domes of the boilers and the turrets sticking out from the ceiling of the shed reminded me of Istanbul. Would this Frontline Parliament also turn out to be as giant a hoax as The Collective? The same brain had concocted both the games. Aatushi finished writing on a brick and pasted it on the wall. Coming back to the stage, she took the mike and announced, 'I have cast my ballot. Later, after we've heard everyone's voice, a committee co-chaired by the HR Director and the Union President will decide conclusively on the issue and declare their decision by tomorrow evening. Once we've agreed to this process, each one of us is obliged to comply with the decision that emerges.' She looked around at every corner of the room catching as many eyes as she could and then concluded for emphasis, 'Including me.' The neon tower came on at that very moment, lending a dramatic touch to the end of her speech.

Loquacious, Pause and I fanned out among the staff to help them. Some people were already writing, others had to have explained to them what to do again, and a third lot who couldn't write had to be helped by penning down their thoughts for them. We urged people to decide their vote individually, not in pairs or small groups, which we explained wasn't how Deep Democracy worked. It wasn't about lobbies and interest groups, as in the case of democracy; rather it was how each individual really felt. And decided. Finally everybody stuck their 'brick' on the wall, the actual wall of the plant building covered by a giant laminate sheet.

By the time the voting was over, the sun was a large ball of fire on the horizon. We counted the 'bricks'; the final figure was 549 from a total of 650 employees across the plant, Head Office, and sales offices (and there were plans to get the regional sales people to vote by phone). Even if the vote went against the VRS, the concept of the Frontline Parliament was a success! Pause and I were elated at the turnout. The new toy worked!

But, as usual, for me doubt followed joy. Like so many times before, I told myself, 'Where's the need for such happiness? All toys finally break, don't they? Or you grow out of them. So every time you see a working toy, look for the flaw that will be its downfall.'

Aloud I asked Pause, 'Suppose the whole lot has voted against the VRS? Where would that leave us?'

Pause didn't reply. She showed me a large group

of egrets, maybe fifty strong, flying past the setting sun in formation. It was a picture-postcard moment and I guessed she was trying to tell me that I should believe in togetherness and beauty.

'Does real life flow from a postcard or is it the other way round?' I asked no one in particular because Pause had drifted away.

A few crows appeared in reply, making a huge racket as they flew raggedly in the opposite direction of the flock that had just made its way north. I looked around for the real-life symbolism of this sighting. Ah, there it was: a handful of workers playing conscientious abstainers, standing in a group just outside the circle of light thrown by the neon tower. They were observing everything closely from the sidelines, but despite Pause's attempts to rope them in they were resisting participation. In a Deep Democracy I had expected the 'Aye' and the 'Nay' sayers but how was one to deal with this group of 'None of the above' sayers?

Pause had moved on by the time I reached the group. When I accosted their leader, a goateed, suave, lanky man with a thin, reedy voice like the high notes of a flute, he told me they would rather wait for their leader Rana's directive before getting involved.

'So, you are his supporters?' I asked the group in Hindi.

'Yes, we invited him to come to Frozen Air when our union wasn't able to represent our case.'

Either Flute had been deputed or had assumed the responsibility to talk on their behalf.

'Do any of you know him?'

'Who doesn't know Rana in these parts?' He looked around at his mates who nodded in agreement.

'Personally, I mean.'

'There's nothing personal in all this. We are here to demand what is our right. And he's the best man to get it for us. We hadn't met him before this… but we've all heard of his exploits.'

'You mean the closure of Heavy Engineering Equipment?'

'The management chickened out.'

'Where did that leave the 60,000 workers and their families? What about ACC? The management gave in to all of Rana's demands. And Srikrishna Pistons? What happened there?' I stared from one face to the other. Each one turned away from me, most looking down at their feet or in the distance.

Flute looked around at his group and spoke, 'We're loyal to our leader, sir. You won't be able to break us. We've put our weight behind him. Now we have no choice. It's loyalty or death.'

Put like that, he didn't give me an option either. I withdrew from the group on the pretext of a call and didn't go back. My enthusiasm at the success of the Frontline Parliament was dampened by this little group's obduracy. There was no doubt that a skirmish, possibly even a battle, was in the offing.

Most likely, the showdown with Rana would come when the committee chaired by Don took the final decision tomorrow based on today's vote. Whatever the decision, there would be a commotion during the announcement because Rana was sure to crash the party then. It would take something really special from Pause to keep things from turning ugly.

CHAPTER 9

The Twist

'No news from Rana yet...' Pause sounded disappointed. Tea had been served at one end of the parachute tent. Pause and I had taken our tea and snacks into the empty canteen. The overhead tube lights weren't switched on yet, though it was almost dark in the giant hall. Only the light from the tall neon lamp outside streamed in through the ventilators and fell in neat rectangles between the tables at the far end, where I took a seat facing the doors. As Pause walked through the rectangles of light, her face alternatively lit up briefly and fell into darkness again, like she was sitting at the window of a train pulling into a sporadically lit platform. Whenever her cheeks suddenly glowed, the translucency of her dusky skin made me think of a water-gorged raisin in its prime.

'No news of Rana...' she repeated, pulling up a chair.

'No news from Rana is good news as far as I am concerned.'

She looked amused at my reaction. Sitting down across the aluminium-topped table she said, 'You don't wish to see Rana again?'

'Unless he's behind bars.'

'Tch, tch, tch! You're being mean now. He called us over to his place, now it's our turn to return the hospitality,' she said. 'And, in any case, not inviting him to our party won't stop him from coming, you know.'

'I know. I was talking to his supporters and they said he's not going to accept the verdict of the Frontline Parliament.' I pushed away my samosa, suddenly not feeling hungry. 'This is dangerous stuff.'

'The samosa? Dangerous?'

'I don't have the stomach for all this unpleasantness.'

'You haven't eaten anything all day.' Her voice softened.

Come to think of it, I hadn't been hungry for a fortnight now. I couldn't remember eating properly, since the mysterious postcard had arrived at my desk.

I watched Pause demolish her samosa in the gathering gloom. Where had she picked up such an appetite for intrigue? Looking into at her calm, innocent eyes one could hardly suspect that a cunning fox lurked behind the façade. Even now, as she chewed contemplatively on her samosa, I could bet she was busy scheming at another twisted plot. I was relieved I had crossed over to her side since yesterday. It also left her free to worry about worthier opponents like Rana.

'Janice is the one who worries me more.' She startled me by her remark, which seemed to indicate she could read what was going on in my head. How did she do that? 'She was furious after the meeting. She came up to me and said in that irritating drawl of hers, "What are you trying to pull with this Frontline Parliament?"' Pause imitated the accent with pouted lips and her head shaking like one of those dolls with a spring for a neck. '"Let me be clear, Pause: layoffs are part of the agreement. If you don't retrench, the deal is off." Then she stomped off without hearing me out. All she wants, like Shylock, is to get her pound of flesh.'

'She quite hates your guts,' I added, to spice things up a bit.

Pause scowled, nodding her head in the affirmative. 'Yup, she's been looking daggers at me ever since we met. Much before the agreement was even drafted. We've crossed swords at every step. I hate her Texan obduracy and she abhors my Malayali deviousness.'

'Have you ever tried to explain your concept of ownership to her?'

'No. But you saw the storm break out on her

face when Aatushi was talking about it. She's feudal down to her little finger. She'll never let control slip out of her hands. She's not ready to hand over decision-making to Aatushi, let alone allowing it to trickle right down to the workers. Under the guise of monitoring, she's been camping here and interfering in everything.' The hall was almost dark, though not as dark as the expression on Pause's face.

'Is there anything in black and white in the agreement about cutting the workforce?'

'No numbers but it's there all right. There's a clause devoted to the "right" kind of skills required and the strategies for acquiring people with those skills.'

'So what happens if the staff says no to the VRS?' Pause's face was frozen into a grimace.

Somebody switched on the rows of tube lights on the wall behind her, which emphasized to me the passing hour and my need for a drink after experiencing almost twenty-four hours of gut-wrenching emotions that had touched the summits of elation and plumbed the depths of despair, sometimes within minutes of each other, like a crazy ride in an amusement park. 'Anyway, we'll see tomorrow…' I pushed my chair back, ready to call it a day.

Suddenly, a smile sprung up on her frigid face like a crocus from under the snow. And then spring arrived! Wild flowers burst forth all over, a bloom of laughter erupted and the thaw was evident. 'Don't go just yet, Sancho. I have a plan.' She looked up at me with a devious glint in her eyes that made my blood clot. I could feel pain and suffering coming my way. Learning, too, which I had been told time and again made it all bearable. But my cup was full of learning and any more would only overflow. And in any case all the insight came only in hindsight. Right now what I could see was my hind in grave danger and I had to get it out of her sight pronto.

'Good for you, Pause. You go ahead; Loquacious is waiting for me at the guest house.' I made a feeble attempt to get up from my chair.

Pause lunged across the table and caught my hand, pulling me down. She drew her face conspiratorially close to mine and said, 'Sancho, help me with Janice no?' I settled back resignedly. 'She has asked me to meet her at 7.00 p.m. in her room at the guest house. Can you meet her instead?'

'Me? Why?'

'I need you to take her to meet Rana.'

'You're mad! Rana? Why should she meet him?'

'I've been thinking. Let's try to broker a deal between the two. She wants the Frontline Parliament to fail; so does Rana. He loses his power if the staff is allowed to decide on the VRS themselves.'

'But Rana and Janice are on the opposite side of the VRS divide. She wants it and he doesn't.'

'For a fee he'll cross any divide. I'm sure she can convince him it's the right thing. What does he care anyway as long as he makes money, one way or the other?'

'But why would you want them allied together? You're up to some games again, Pause…'

'The whole of human civilization is one big game. I'm betting when you put both of them together on the same side, they'll cancel each other out.'

'You're betting on the wrong guy to be the broker. After last night, I'm public enemy no. 1 for Rana! And why should Janice trust me either?'

'Well, it was your remark, which gave me the idea.'

'It did? What remark?'

'You said the staff might reject the VRS in the Frontline Parliament, didn't you? You sounded disappointed about it. So, you go to her and say you're against my jeopardizing the VRS through the Frontline Parliament. You are, aren't you? In your heart of hearts? You drafted the scheme, after all.'

I shook my head vehemently.

'Are you denying you made it?' she asked, turning all innocent.

'No, I'm not. But I don't think I have a problem… forget it, I don't want to think at all.'

'Then do as I say. Please, Sancho. It's for the good of Frozen Air.'

I turned my face towards the window. Darkness was spreading its tentacles over the world and one of the limbs crept right into my heart. I shivered involuntarily.

Beyond the dubious morality of her plan, the prospect of another visit to the lion's den was terrifying. 'Rana was ready to kill me yesterday. He hasn't had a change of heart for sure. Then why are you pushing me like a sacrificial goat in front of him?'

'Well, you were ready to kill me till yesterday. I'm only returning the favour.' She got up and walked over to the sink. 'Don't worry…' she reassured me as we washed our hands. 'Once he sees the American he'll have no time for you, believe me.'

'I don't see the point of all this,' I said in a frustrated tone of voice. 'Why throw your two greatest enemies together?' I turned away, shaking my head, and walked out of the canteen ahead of her.

Acting according to Pause's script, I got Flute to arrange a meeting between Rana and Janice at 8.00 p.m. that night. When I met her at seven and offered my assistance to her, she was willing to listen but wasn't exactly enthusiastic.

'Uh, huh. Go on Sanshit…'

I winced as usual at the way she pronounced my name, even while noting the veracity in her statement. I hadn't cleared my bowels for two days now. Maybe because I had hardly eaten anything for so long except of course my words, Don's bullshit, my pride — and now it was time to eat humble pie.

'You know what, you have been like a breath of fresh air in our frozen firm. You've breathed life into a dying organization. For the first time I feel like my performance is of any consequence.' I meant every word, specially the bit about my performance. 'Now, just when I think we are on the right path, the Frontline Parliament is there to block the way. I believe in worker empowerment but this is way over the top. It's an abdication of the management's responsibility. Why does a manager get paid so much higher than a worker?'

'I hear you Sanshit,' she said, not wanting to react before she'd heard my entire story.

'A manager has better knowledge and skills and therefore he can take more informed decisions. How can you hand over decision-making to the uneducated masses? That's why every nation needs an elite intelligentsia to rule. Even a communist one!'

'I agree,' she said, still tentative.

'So, when I heard from the HR Director you weren't exactly in support of Pause's mad scheme, I thought I'd find you and talk with you.'

'Here I am. Go ahead, you can talk to me.'

'Also, if the staff have voted out the VRS in that stupid Parliament, we are in a soup. The company needs a VRS.'

'It owes me a VRS, Sanshit. We signed on it.'

'I have a plan, ma'am.'

'Call me Janice.'

'Janice, I say let's enlist Rana's support to ruin Pause's plans.'

The American knitted her brow, rolling the idea over in her handsome head. I held my breath and watched the mole on her lip bounce around like a yoyo. After a while, she pursed her lower lip and covered the mole with it. Her plucked eyebrows lifted into perfect arches. She said, 'That may work! It may actually work! I might've misread you. I thought you were… you were somewhat simple. And on *her* side. Joining me is the best thing you could have done. We are right back in the reckoning. Missy, watch out. Here come Sanshit and Janice!' she shouted, holding out her hand to me.

These Americans, I tell you! They reduce everything to a comic book. She was behaving as if we were Robin and Poison Ivy on a mission to get Batwoman.

Mustn't forget The Joker while we were at it. 'And Rana,' I said, shaking her extended hand.

'Him too. How do we contact the guy?'

'We'll have to go over to his place, of course.' Seeing some reluctance, I added, 'I was there yesterday.'

'Hmm… I know. You're a brave guy. To want to do this two nights running.'

'Tonight, you'll have to do the talking, though,' I clarified.

'Well, then, why can't I talk to him on the phone?'

'On the phone he won't understand your Texan drawl, for sure. His English is pretty challenged. We could do a conference call with me translating but in our country we do deals in person. There's an advance involved, you see. A pretty hefty sum.'

'How much?'

'I haven't spoken to him directly but we'd better take a thick wad.'

'I haven't got that much in rupees.'

'Seeing where the rupee has climbed against the dollar, the latter may be a better bet for you. But I wonder if he'll accept dollars.'

'He'll come around,' she said with pouted lips and a wink, which I didn't know what to make of.

Despite my education on women's psychology through Bills and Moon, I still have a long way to go. I didn't pick up her drift even when I came to pick Janice up, though I did notice she'd changed into Indian clothes for the occasion. She had on a bright yellow kurta and black salwar, which enhanced her pale features somehow. The shade of her lipstick was almost black, matching the colour of the salwar.

As soon as we got into the car, bound for Rana's farmhouse, we began to write the storyboard for the evening. I wanted to finish this discussion before we reached the canal road. The town of Surajpur was turning in for the night. Driving past the main bazaar, we found most of the shutters already down, though there was still quite a bit of traffic. I told her all I knew about Rana's past, his politics and his sexual escapades. The last seemed to titillate her no end and she had many questions about Rana's exploits, to which I had no answers.

Finally, when she asked me hopefully, 'Will he try to hit on me or something?' I began to see what she'd been getting at.

'I have only experienced him trying to hit me with a bullet,' I answered honestly.

'Is he good-looking?' She sounded like a teenager on a blind date. She had obviously set her heart on seducing him, somehow believing this would get her a better deal. I didn't have the heart to spoil her party just then, though I knew her picture of Rana as a provincial cowboy was set to shatter soon. And why fool around with pictures when she was set to meet the real specimen, though he wouldn't let her miss his larger-than-life pictures in that long corridor.

'He looks quite ferocious actually.'

'Really? I like strong men.'

I had had enough of this coquetry and changed the topic to matters of substance. I suggested to her, 'The Frontline Parliament results are to be declared in the evening tomorrow. We should urge Rana to arrange a gate meeting just after that.'

'Shouldn't it be before? That way he can rubbish the Parliament and not have to bother with the result. Yes, let's ask him to do the gate meeting before the Parliament results are announced.'

'Uh... sure...' I said, though, actually, I was very unsure whether the timing would suit Pause because I knew she was keen to have the results announced first.

'He can have the meeting at the end of the first shift, around two! Tell me Sanshit, what's this Rana guy's position on the VRS? Can we get him to speak for it?'

'It's possible. He's used to switching sides like a flipped coin. Always for a substantial fee, though.'

'I am willing to pay but will he be able to deliver? What if he's all bluster?'

'To be frank that's all I have seen of him. I saw a lot of his wrath yesterday but it was all bark. Now it's time to test his bite.'

As we parked outside Rana's mansion, the wrath I had spoken of earlier was conspicuous by its absence. Instead, a carnival seemed to be on: flags of India and the USA fluttered from his gatepost; the gates we'd found so menacing the last time round were festooned with garlands of marigold and rose. 'Born in the USA' was being piped through loudspeakers.

Where had Stepney laid hands on the tape, the flag and the flowers so quickly? He'd acquired a cheap suit too. Attired in it now, with his beard and hair well combed, he welcomed us at the gate with a 100-watt smile. As we neared, he climbed atop a stool, and looking us proudly in the eye put a tilak on our foreheads and garlands around our necks. A rude push of the thumb as he anointed my forehead was the only hint of rancour from last night.

I was surprised to see old man Rana himself greet us at the front porch. He had been standing there all the time watching us cross his large front yard. We had just climbed the porch, when he exploded in broken English, 'Hay! How dee? You first Amrikan in my home!'

I veered to the side and feasted my eyes on Rana's makeover: his thin chocolate brown tie, white bowler hat and brown alligator skin shoes reminded me of a style made famous by Ajit, a popular villain of Bollywood films of the seventies.

Suddenly he bent over and grabbed Janice's hand to kiss it. He couldn't actually touch his lips to the hand, though, for his moustache came in the way, prompting the American to snatch her hand back in alarm. My skin crawled when I tried to imagine what it must have felt like to have Rana's moustache caress the back of her hand. Like accidentally picking up a hedgehog. She withdrew her hand with such force that she lurched backwards, and was teetering at the edge of the porch. If I hadn't steadied her with my arm from behind, she might have fallen; but at my touch, and in the circumstances you couldn't blame her for being as skittish as an unbroken horse, she

jumped forward into Rana's arms. Rana wasn't one
to look a gift horse in the mouth. He embraced her
unconditionally, muttering blissfully, 'Amrikans very
fast!'

With a look of undisguised disgust on her face
(luckily Rana being near blind, missed it), she
stepped away, brushing her salwar down. I can
conclusively say that all the traces of coquettishness
from earlier in the evening had vanished by this early
stage of the meeting.

To divert Rana's attention away from her, I put
forward my hand tentatively to shake hands with
him but he pointedly ignored me. He turned around
and waited for us to step alongside. When we were
abreast of him, he crooked his elbow; the American
slipped in her hand hesitantly, looking towards me
for encouragement. Going with the mood of things, I
gestured to her to cover her head with her chunni like
a demure Hindu bride. She complied with a fierce
look in her eyes. I sensed she was beginning to lose
her patience with the charade.

Our gang moved towards the durbar hall in
slow motion and I admired the odd couple thrown
together by Pause from the vantage point of a side
actor in the unfolding drama. Floating along the
corridor at the speed of a pole-propelled boat in the
backwaters of Kerala, Rana pointed out the sights
that consisted in the main of the Bollywood-style
posters we'd seen earlier depicting him as the hero

of the various stories of his chequered life. Halfway
through the passage, the American looked back at
me, exasperated, and I gestured for her to tug at his
elbow to move the boat faster through the channel.
After that it was Janice towing Rana's boat the rest of
the way. If it upset Rana, he didn't show it.

'Very fast Amrikans!' He repeated a couple of
times, letting her lead.

In the durbar hall, another smaller throne was
placed in front of Rana's. The American sat down on
it gingerly, her buttocks cantilevered precariously at
the edge.

Rana asked, 'Have you hear of my cock's-tale,
madam? Very famous.'

'What?' She was visibly frazzled. Even the blind
Rana noticed the frown on her face and the tone of
her voice.

'Then what you have?'

'He's asking if you want a drink or something,' I
butted in to calm her down. I was sitting on one of
the courtiers' chairs while the boys stood on either
side of Rana.

'Nah!' she exploded. She added under her breath
but loud enough for me to hear, 'For Chrissake, let's
get on with it...'

But Rana wasn't done with the foreplay yet. 'No
cock's-tale? Maybe, Amrikan ladies like it straight. I
have hard on too, huh?' He chuckled.

'Look, pal, I am here on clean business. If you're

interested in a deal, let's talk. Else, I'm outta here.'
When she got a blank look from Rana at her outburst,
she sighed and said, 'Can I use the ladies' room?'

'Which room you want?'

Sheepishly, I cleared my throat and spoke to Rana
for the first time that night, 'Bathroom...'

'Ah.' Rana motioned with his little finger upright
to one of his boys to accompany her there.

She gestured violently with her thumb at me. I
jumped up to conduct her through to the only loo I
knew, at the other end of the small room where they'd
held Don. When she saw the mirrors and the satin-
sheeted beds in Rana's love nest, she lost it, 'Look at
this sleaze pit. He's a dirty old man! Let's get outta
here! Abort mission, Sanshit.'

'Easy, ma'am. It's hard on you, I understand but
you have to ignore his libido; we need him!'

'Hard on me, yes, thank you! What did he mean back
there?'

'Oh that? He was just asking you whether you'd
like any hard liquor – whisky, vodka and the likes. As
against his cocktails for which he claimed he's famous
in the region.'

'Uh!' A visibly relieved Janice Kramer moved
towards the toilet.

As she opened the door, I said, 'Once you show
him the money, his lust will come to heel. I can bet
he'll quietly tuck his libido between his legs and start
talking business.'

Reflecting on my suggestion, she disappeared into the loo to powder her nose while I waited for her in the sleaze den. She was in there for a fair while, enough for me to make a call to Pause reporting our progress thus far. She was satisfied except about the timing of Rana's gate meeting. She was categorical about that: I should insist on 6.00 p.m. after the Frontline Parliament results had been declared.

Janice still hadn't come out when I finished talking to Pause. It was getting too complicated. Janice trying to keep her cool; Rana trying to seduce her; Pause trying to fix both of them; and I in the middle of it all trying to manage the protagonists. I suddenly realized I was no side actor in this drama, I was one of its directors. I wished I had a clearer script to see me through.

'I am going home!' I shouted to myself in the broken mirror of the bedroom.

'Don't leave me here alone,' a terrified Janice said over the noise of the flush as she walked out of the washroom.

I assured her it was only a phrase, a manner of speaking, and I wouldn't dream of leaving her in the lion's den. She looked doubtful as we walked back in to be greeted by a salacious wink from Rana and a remark in Hindi, 'Took your time. Bit old for you isn't she?'

'Mature women like younger men,' I replied, also in Hindi, blinking both my eyes at him.

He hissed like a pressure cooker releasing his frustrations of last night. 'Don't get fresh with me, you motherfucker! She's old enough to be your mom.'

To his credit, he noticed the alarm in the American's eyes and calmed down immediately. He said, 'That boy – yesterday enemy, today friend. In business, as in politics, everybody is friend.' I wasn't convinced; a bullet with my name on it nestled in one of the boys' guns. 'Anyhow, let us business,' he shifted gear. 'Who are you?'

'That's none of your business, Mister Rayna Veedraw Badodour Sing. What I want you to do for me I can tell you.'

'Whaat? No foreplay. You want to do right away.' Rana laughed at his own joke.

The American took a deep breath and made, by the looks of it, one last attempt. 'Sorry to spoil your party, Mister Badodour, but I'm cutting right to the climax.' She brought out a large wad of 100-dollar bills and thumped it down on the table emphatically. I was impressed with her resourcefulness. She'd produced a substantial sum at a very short notice. The new notes glinted in the light of the massive chandelier. Rana pretended to ignore the wad though his two boys, provincial goons at heart, couldn't resist. They bent towards the table for a closer look.

'Okay, your deal madam. I'll cut.' Rana picked up the pack and said disappointedly, 'Not much!'

I intervened, 'Rana-ji, that is dollars. Not rupees.'

'Ah!' He brought them really close. My guess was he'd never really seen a dollar bill before.

'One dallar equals about 50 ruepees. So this is ten lakh ruepees,' she explained it as she might to a nine-year-old. 'One-tenth of the amount if you can help me win the game.' Janice sounded comfortable now. Constructing deals was her home turf.

'What game we play?'

She turned towards me and asked, 'What time is the result of the Frontline Parliament going to be declared?'

'Five p.m.'

'Mister Badodour, at two you shall hold a gate meeting where you shall "persuade" the workers to reject the Frontline Parliament using whatever means are available to you.'

'Frontline Parliament? What is? Only Parliament I know Lok Sabha and Rajya Sabha.'

'Something the new management has set up to facilitate decision-making by the workers,' I explained.

'Decision-making by workers? What nonsense? What happens to us? Bad idea. Take democracy too far, the people stand on your head and piss.'

'I agree.' She looked at me to convey this part was going well. 'Very dangerous stuff we're playing with here. Anyway, all ya got to do is rubbish it completely sayin' that no such Parliament will be allowed here in this region.'

'What you ask is my playsure. I eat cake and keep the icing. Great people think like. Our waves right length. Madam, let us drink to aaver jodi...'

'Hang in there, mister. Hear the entire deal before you get all excited. What I've asked of you till now is only the icing. Here comes the cake. In the same meeting you have to put your considerable weight behind the VRS.'

'I know only far or against. What behind?'

'She means in favour of the VRS,' I clarified in Hindi.

He was a veteran of many games; he didn't even flinch as he weighed the task in his mind. 'Cost you high, madam. Five per cent of total VRS amount.'

Ooh! He had a price list. He'd obviously batted for a VRS before. I did a quick calculation. The sum he was asking for could be anything between two and five crores. I looked over at Janica to see whether she had anticipated such a high payoff.

'Three per cent, not a payeesa more,' she said as if she were bargaining for potatoes with a vegetable vendor.

'Three per cent? Hmmm... okay. Plus eye operation at Shroff Clinic in Delhi. All expense include business-class ticket.'

'Done.'

I looked on in awe at the breathtaking display of bargaining I had just witnessed.

'So Mr Badodour Sing, your goal is to cajole the people to accept the VRS.'

'Kajol, not my type. I like... mmm...' He looked up, thinking.

She interrupted his search for a Bollywood heroine of his choice. 'Fine if you don't like cajole, coerce if necessary – the VRS must go through!'

'Course?' He looked at me.

'She means force.'

Rana broke into a grin. 'You are woman after my heart...'

She put out her hand signifying the end of our meeting. 'Rest when your job is done...'

He looked at her lustily, 'Uhnnh! I love strong laundiyas.'

The American withdrew her hand hastily and put it on her heart. I could feel her breathing heavily as I quickly steered her out. Outside, Stepney was nowhere to be seen. The Springsteen tape had run out and we hurried towards the car in the eerie stillness of the night.

Once in the car, her body began to shake, all colour drained out of her face and the mole started a wild jitterbug. The head of Mcsinki, principal shareholder in many firms, she, who'd bankrupted scores of firms, axed thousands of employees, ordered dozens of executions, had the shivers; I sensed it would take her a long time to recover from her meeting with Rana. At the same time, I noticed the hint of a smile

as well. The global cowgirl had not only withstood
the provincial outlaw, she'd made a deal with him.
To her it must have felt like she'd played with fire and
got away without getting burnt.

CHAPTER 10

The Coup

If Aatushi's debut had been well attended, then the old favourite Rana's show could be declared sold out. Not only was he a reputed orator, but word had also spread of his promise of 'revenge', drawing in not only the entire staff of Frozen Air but also the families of the workmen and even neighbouring villagers in droves.

The crowd had been building up since noon in an open field outside the factory gate; they came from all over in buses, bullock carts and on foot. It was an unusually warm February day but there was no hint of it on the faces of the people squatting calmly in front of an embankment, patiently waiting for Rana's entry. A contingent of policemen (requested by the management), thirty strong, lazed about smoking bidis and swapping stories in the shade of the factory wall some distance away.

Pause and I stood in the guardhouse at the factory gate watching the crowd with powerful binoculars through a window in the outer wall. The security superintendent, a seventy-year-old ex-naik subedar from the Indian Army, who's room we were in, sat at a huge desk at the far end away from the gate, writing fiercely on a sheet of paper.

'Tch, the timing is wrong... if the workers had heard the results of their vote ...' Pause said worriedly.

This nervousness from the eternal optimist wasn't a good sign. I surreptitiously squeezed her hand. I clarified my position yet again. 'I couldn't do anything. Janice was clear: either the meeting is before the results of the Parliament are announced or not at all.'

'Whose side are they on? What do you think?' She looked out at the crowd.

The superintendent stopped writing and replied cheerfully, 'It's a huge gathering... with the VRS issue not yet conclusively addressed Rana has the upper hand.'

She said, 'I wasn't asking about the crowd. I meant the police.'

'Oh, you can never tell till the action starts. But one thing is for sure, Rana isn't going to try a stunt like the one he pulled three days ago. He won't dare enter the place. The HR Director himself went and met the Superintendent of Police in the morning. And

I'm writing a pre-emptory request to have the force placed here for a fortnight or so.'

'Good. I wanted to ask you another thing. Rana's got everybody wondering what industrial action he has up his sleeve... What's the worst he can do? Legally?'

'A strike, I guess. Though it's the non-industrial action we should all be worried about.' He shrugged as he said this.

At half-past-two, just when I was beginning to doubt whether Rana was coming at all, two jeeps veered off the road. They tore across the field at breakneck speed to the embankment, leaving in their wake an ominous cloud of dust.

Rana Vidroh Bahadur Singh had arrived. I focused my binoculars on him. There was no mistaking his belligerent mood – his moustache was like two pistols joined at the barrels under his nose. Gunmen dotted the open jeeps like oranges on a tree.

Rana made his intentions clear soon after disembarking. Taking Pockmark's AK47 he fired a volley into the air to underline his arrival. The policemen with their ancient .303 rifles looked on enviously at the gun that was capable of spitting out justice so rapidly and accurately. Their officer ordered them to stop gawking and move closer to the crowd.

I looked at Pause worriedly, 'Have we bitten off more than we can chew?'

Pause squeezed my hand reassuringly and said, 'Only when you bite off more than you can chew do you realize how strong your jaw really is.'

'I just get a bad stomach ache, is all.'

Rana was scowling as he limped up to the embankment leaning on the boys' shoulders, one on either side of him. He stood at the bottom of the steep incline, probably wondering how to negotiate it. It looked like an insurmountable obstacle unless the two bodyguards carried him up, except that would undermine his alpha male reputation in front of his constituency. While I was speculating on what he would do, Rana took a sudden ferocious leap and scrambled up the slope to the mike on his own. Wow! The adrenalin must be gushing from the old man's gland like water from a dam's open sluice gates.

He looked around imperiously at the large gathering, nodding at a group here, waving at another. Grabbing the mike, he spoke in chaste Hindi.

'Did you know this factory is slated to close down soon? Did you know that? My sources tell me the gases we make here are polluting, to be phased out soon as per an international agreement. The kaminas have been disrobing the place like she was Draupadi and we don't even know it.' He was known for peppering his speech as liberally with choice abuses as with allusions to the *Mahabharata*. 'Poisonous gases are being produced in our backyard by these chutiyas for decades; our environment, our soil is tainted.

Either you or someone from your family, working for these Kauravs from Delhi, has helped them do it to her. Why do you sit like Dhrithrashtra, pretending to be blind to their games? Why have none of you raised a voice until now? They've stripped her naked and you sit there dumbly. Why did no one tell me before? Luckily the rape is not yet complete. And now that I know of their dirty designs, I won't let it happen! Not in my backyard! I will save Draupadi's honour!' His claws were out, his teeth bared and his roar deafening.

'Clever line to take. He's smarter than I thought.' Pause took the binoculars from me and trained them on Rana.

'I say it again: you're blind, you fools! Take this Parliament the new management has constituted. It's unconstitutional. The only Parliament for this region lies in the state capital. And I, Rana Bahadur Singh, represent all of you there. Anything else is illegal, against the constitution. It's a dishonour to me. The other night, they even tried to shame me in my own sanctum sanctorum. Some impudent puppies belonging to the new management of this factory came and tried to make a deal with me. But I am not for sale, you chutiyas! Rana can't be bought or sold. Not respecting my stature is like spitting on all of you and the whole region.

'This Parliament they say will take all the decisions. What nonsense? Never heard of such an arrangement. I say it's a sham. A means of blaming it all on you later when the factory is closed down. They will tell you that you took the decisions, which led to the closure.'

I looked away from him at Pause next to me. 'Wrong bowler to bring on at this stage, Pause. He's all set to bowl out the Frontline Parliament. Calling him here through Janice was like hitting your own wickets. I still don't know what you were thinking when you pitched the two of them together.'

Pause, her eyes glued to the binoculars, didn't reply.

Rana thundered on. 'For decades they treat you like slaves, now suddenly they want you to become owners. Poppycock! Kaminas are playing a huge trick, I say. If they want you to be real owners then they should give you money to start your own business. Real money. Not the peanuts they're offering in the VRS. And while we are on the topic of the VRS; my stand on it is simple: Double the VRS amount.'

'Should have guessed it!' Pause blurted out. 'The higher the amount, the bigger his percentage share.'

'And I want each jackass here to take the VRS. Do you hear? Consider yourself volunteered.'

'The higher the number of people who opt for it, the more he gets.' I shook my head, waiting for the mayhem to begin.

'Keep your factory, you chutiyas, I say to the management! Give us the VRS. Anyway you'll close down in a year or two. Then what happens to us? Why not we take the money and become owners of our own small businesses? Keep your dying business. Good riddance to the polluting factory. Here's my final offer to you. Double the VRS now! We'll take it. To a man!' He motioned to his goons and the squad let loose shots in the air. 'Today, as you can see, I am in no mood for speeches. I want action. Here's my proposal. Let's gherao the bloody place, till they agree to our demand.'

The rallying cry was taken up by a section of the crowd. 'Gherao! Gherao!'

'What exactly is a gherao?' Pause asked me innocently.

'You don't know?' I screamed. Seeing alarm on the face of the security superintendent, I piped down to a fierce whisper. 'He is planning to encircle us. Lay a goddamn siege to the factory! It couldn't get worse than this! The MD's daughter, the HR Director and the entire top management are in the plant today. We've handed him the best day in years for a gherao.'

'Could it turn violent?'

'Do you have a hanky?' She shook her head. 'You bet it can. Seeing Rana's mood and firepower this one has plenty of potential to turn ugly. He's going to get his goons to enter the place like they did the other day

and rough up some of our officers to make sure. Then
seal the place. We could be inside for days.'

'What about the cops?'

'This ragtag battalion of provincial policemen
can't stand up to his army. And looks like many of
the workers will take his side.'

'He'll have to ask them at least, won't he?'

'Sure, but he's not going to waste time with subtle
methods like the secret ballot we'd employed in the
Frontline Parliament yesterday.'

I was proved right by the ultimatum he gave the
workmen.

'All those not in favour of this proposal can get
up and walk back to work.' Rana threw the challenge
cleverly.

Pause said, 'He's loaded the choice in his favour.
Nobody will dare make that long walk. Consider how
brave anyone opposed to Rana's proposal would have
to be: he would have to stand up, turn his back on
Rana and his goons, walk past the squatting workers
who are for the motion, across the field, up to the
gate almost fifty metres away. The distance would
take maybe three minutes to cover and all along he
would be totally exposed, ready for the picking by
Rana's goons.'

Ten seconds ticked by. No one moved. No one
spoke.

I had been mingling with the workers since Rana
had announced his gate meeting this morning and

many had told me they wouldn't dare to mess with Rana. They had their families to think of. Some had indicated they were willing to give the Frontline Parliament a chance but it was clear no one was ready to vote for it with their feet. Their reaction might have made them seem ready to swallow the bitter VRS pill, but I knew that for many the pill was going down facilitated by large gulps of fear.

Half a minute had gone since he'd thrown his dare; still nobody stirred. Rana's face broke into a smile for the first time that afternoon. With no apparent challenge to his proposition, things seemed to be going according to script for him.

Just when we had all given up hope, with a sudden clang, the factory gates opened; as the crowd, the goons and the policemen turned towards the gate, the February afternoon turned with them. For a while, we, in the guardroom couldn't see who it was, for the angle was too acute. But I recognized the voice that boomed across the field towards Rana. 'Hey, Nana, you badmash! Wait for me!'

It was Don! All eyes except mine were on the diminutive figure stepping in mincing yet confident steps towards the crowd. I took the binoculars from Pause and directed them on Rana's face. His expression of shock, as if a cannonball had landed

with a thud at his feet, gave me the first whiff of
relief from the oppressive heat of the afternoon. And
a cloud of self-doubt scurrying across Rana's face
reinforced the relief.

I turned my binoculars on the diminutive figure
of Don. He was striding purposefully but languidly
towards the crowd, his pants tucked into his boots.
Pause asked for the binoculars at this point.

Stepney, the dwarf, had appeared from one of the
jeeps, running up to the gathering as if his favourite
hero had come on the scene. I said, 'Look at Stepney
wagging his tail. He loves Don.'

Pause didn't smile. She trained the binoculars
on the lone figure about to enter the crowd; in a
horrified whisper she said, 'What's the crazy fool up
to? Hope he doesn't get hurt.'

Don nodded here, waved there, and greeted
workers as if he were on an evening stroll and
had found them all squatting there. He reached
the embankment in minutes and sprang lightly
onto it and stood shoulder to chest besides Rana. I
could see him grinning from ear to ear without the
binoculars.

Pockmark picked a pistol out of his waistband
and aimed it at Don's head but Rana gestured to him
and he kept it back immediately. Rana might have
secretly hoped the management had agreed to his
demand and that Don was coming over to convey
that to him. In any case, he could afford to give the

scatterbrained gasbag a chance to put his wares in front of the public, who were now eating out of Rana's hand.

The HR Director took the mike and said, 'Hello, Nana. I see you've gathered my workers together. Now that you have finished your charming little speech, may I use your mike to address them?' Don didn't wait for permission; he continued talking, his booming voice coming across the sound system as impressively as Rana's.

'It saves me the trouble of calling a meeting. I was listening to you from inside. I salute your respect for Draupadi's honour and the true words you spoke about the pollution from this factory until now. Nana, we graciously accept our folly in producing poisonous gases but they weren't aimed at this region. We helped to create a faraway hole in the sky that threatens the entire planet and not just this region, boss. Anyway, once we realized these gases were dangerous for us all, we decided to do something about it. Whichever badmash reported to you that the factory would close down soon, obviously gave you half the information. Yes, the old gases and the old technology will have to go, but at the same time we have entered into an agreement to bring in new technology for non-polluting refrigerant gases.'

The workers knew about this from Aatushi's speech yesterday but the rest of the public began to murmur among themselves at the revelation.

'Also, this VRS of ours has been giving you sleepless nights, hasn't it? So, you'll be very interested to hear an announcement I have to make. You see, on the matter of the VRS we had a kind of election yesterday; about 550 people voted.' He turned away from Rana to look at the crowd. 'Thanks for your tremendous participation, friends. Now, the results are out. I was going to announce them in the evening but when I saw my friend here had taken so much trouble to gather you together, I thought I might as well use this opportunity. So, friends... An overwhelming majority of you has voted FOR THE VRS, as pasted on your notice board: 73.4 per cent of you want the VRS as it is being offered now.' He clapped but no one joined in. 'The People Decisions Committee, which I chaired, agrees with you that we should go ahead with the VRS! Nana, you want that too, right?'

Rana looked at Don, unsure of what was going on. The people wanted the VRS in its current form. The management, too. Where did that leave his gherao? Rana's face broke into a sweat.

'But it's a VRS with a difference. Acting on a suggestion from one of you, the R in VRS has been changed from Retirement to Resignation. Starting tomorrow everybody, including the CEO, will resign from their posts voluntarily. You will get the entire VRS amount due to you. Not double, as Nana here has suggested. Don't lose your shirt just yet, Nana. At the same time, each of you will get a fresh one-year contract with the company. During this year, as we absorb the new technologies, we will all try to learn the skills required of us with the full support of the management. You'll get no salary for the year but lots of training. At the end of the year, whoever makes the grade will be re-appointed, the contracts of the rest will not be renewed. And we will submit their fate to the Frontline Parliament next year.'

The crowd broke out into whispered conversations. I snatched the binoculars from Pause. Rana's transformation was remarkable. I could swear his proud phallic nose looked flaccid now, and also two inches smaller than normal. Rivulets of sweat had sprung up all over his face, drenching his moustache, which had come unstarched and was hanging straight down past his chin like soggy strands of cotton, somewhat like Fu Manchu, a Chinese villain from a martial arts movie.

'So, friends, we stay married,' Don pressed his advantage, 'but we test the strength of our bond with this one-year contract. Retirement would have meant instant divorce for too many of us. Resignation, training for the new times, and then a year later new marriage vows is a chance given to us by the Frontline Parliament. And that's where I disagree with you, Nana. Please don't ask us to scrap the Parliament. Pretty please. Be a good boy. I believe it is the institution of the future and I'm proud we tried it first in our company. Okay, enough talk. Now

I am going to walk back to the factory. I'd like my
harem to accompany me back to the barracks. Come
with me, my distressed damsels, and let's get back
to work. We have so much to do and so little time.
People from all shifts should report to Sanchit Mishra
in the conference room to submit their resignation
letter and specify their preferences on the training
schedule for next year. And once you've done that,
all those in the second and general shifts please
report to the shop floor. NOW! We don't have time
to waste, friends. Just one year, and so much to learn!
If you are keen on hearing more of the Nana, as I
am, you can do so at a function tomorrow on this
very ground when we gather to formally launch the
Frontline Parliament.' He fluttered his eyelids at Rana
and smiled. 'You'll come, Nana? Won't you? You can
be our chief guest. Same time, same place, boss. And
bring your friends too.'

With that he handed the mike back to a stunned
Rana and jumped off the embankment into the
crowd. He picked his way delicately through the
squatting people; when he reached the edge, he
looked back at them enticingly and beckoned to them
with one crooked finger to follow him.

Nobody got up. The guillotine of the VRS had been
dismantled and the mass execution transformed into
a qualified pardon but they would still have to learn
new tricks for one year without a salary. Also, there
was Rana; how would he respond to Don's little

speech? Rana looked over at his boys in a signal to let the guns do the talking from here on. The boy with the pockmarks picked up his rifle to shoot the tiny figure making his way across the field. Looking through the sights of his rifle he aimed for Don's head. After his escape the other night, which had made their gang the laughing-stock of the region, Pockmarks wanted revenge. He waited anxiously for the final order.

'Fire!' Rana barked. At that exact moment, another figure appeared in Pockmarks' sights, blocking the way. It was Flute; he'd got up, turned his back on Rana and was following Don. Pockmarks cursed and moved the gun slightly to get Don back in his cross hairs but another figure was now obscuring Don from his view. It was Ram Jag. Exasperated, Pockmarks shifted his rifle again but somebody else came between him and the HR Director. Something was wrong! He lowered his gun to see wave upon wave of Frozen Air workers flowing in the direction of the small Pied Piper, who never looked back once, so supremely confident was he of his following. It was as if an ocean was on the march.

From the window in the guardhouse, Pause and I saw a sea of hope rise to Rana's challenge, turn its back on him and flow back towards its own shore. It was a massive homecoming.

Rana's henchmen fell into a single file, their rifles on the ready. They waited for a signal from him to start mowing down the deserters. I shuddered at the thought of a Jallianwallah Bagh-style massacre. Luckily Rana had more sense than General Dyer and knew when the battle was lost. Or was it the police contingent rushing forward to cordon off the mass of workers from the gunmen that fobbed him off?

Whatever it was, it was a historic February afternoon recounted in the folklore of the region as the day ownership overcame fear. Pause had tears streaming down her cheeks. I was crying openly, too, and hugged her with all my might, not bothering about the security inspector's strange looks. Then I rushed to the gate to welcome my victorious Don Quixote.

'What a turnaround, boss!' I exulted as Don reached the gate, reaching out towards him.

Without breaking his stride, Don took out a tiny kerchief from his pocket and handed it to me. 'Wipe your tears, man. There's work to be done.' And he walked past me.

Pause had come running after me and, wiping her tears with the back of her hand, she whispered something in my ear. On Pause's bidding, I ran to catch up with Rana. I stopped him just as he was getting into his jeep. His forlorn face and limp whiskers told the story of his defeat.

I commiserated with him on the rout. He let loose an invective but his heart wasn't in it. I let his frustration run dry in the sandy wastes of the empty field.

Then I informed him, in as sombre a tone as I could muster above the din of all those firecrackers bursting in my heart, 'You were set up, Rana. The American planned it so you would make a fool of yourself.'

'No!' He summoned up his last reserves and sprayed the field with a fresh burst of scathing unprintable invective.

'Yes! Even I was fooled. Behind our backs she had conspired with the HR Director to disrupt your meeting. I saw them talking animatedly inside the gates before he walked out of the plant,' I lied expertly.

'The bitch. I'll make her pay for it.'

'It's a slur against India, what she's done!' I backed out, convinced I had done enough to hasten the Mcsinki head's passage back to Delhi.

I had underestimated the 'Rana effect' because when I told her Rana was baying for her blood and only the presence of the cops was keeping him from entering the plant, she bolted from a side door and went back to New York on a flight that very night.

Epilogue

Within a month of the Frontline Parliament's successful trial, Pause turned down a proposal for marriage from Loquacious. He came to me broken by her sudden 'betrayal'. In deference to his delicate condition, I didn't enlighten him about the changes in the relationship Pause and I shared by then.

He moved on from Frozen Air soon after, though he could never really move on from Pause. I am not sure whether it was Pause's desertion that triggered his depression or whether Godfather's departure from Frozen Air a little earlier was responsible for it; probably it was one coming on the heels of the other that became too much for him to take and it was all downhill after that.

Throughout his slide, ill-luck dogged him like a shadow. Three companies closed down within years of his joining them, and though he may not have been entirely responsible, inevitably he had to shoulder a large part of the blame for he was in very senior positions when they shut shop. And while he was ruining his career, a couple of 'serious' relationships fermented, brewing up a drinking habit that landed him with a debilitating undiagnosed illness. Each time he stood up from a fall, something else tripped him up making him tumble to a level lower. He lurched from hospital to job and back for another five years, when an uncle took pity on him and funded his trip to a well-known sanatorium near Yosemite National Park in California.

Around the same time I, too, took a sabbatical and went off to the University of California, Los Angeles. Whenever I got time from my work, I would meet Loquacious in the sanatorium and usually we'd share a bottle of forbidden wine. The building in which he had a residential quarter bordered a small 5000-year-old sequoia grove. Sitting on the deck outside his room, it was a treat to watch these massive trees huddled together whispering secrets from the past millenia.

In comparison, our talk was only a decade old. And invariably it veered around to what Loquacious was fond of calling the prime of our time at Frozen Air. Our favourite period, of course, was the eventful fortnight leading up to Pause and Don's dramatic triumph over Janice Kramer and Rana Vidroh Bahadur Singh. At times like these, it was not uncommon for goose bumps to appear on our arms like a colony of moles nosing their way through the earth. What electrifying memories they were, bursting right through our skin into the present.

'Do you know where Don Quixote washed up finally?' Loquacious asked me one evening.

'Nope. But I sure hope he got married.'

On the spur of the moment, just for a lark, thinking Don's story might cheer up Loquacious, I switched on my laptop meaning to look for Don on the Internet.

'Nothing like the web to catch truant flies.'

While it was coming on, I rubbed my hands to ward off the cold. 'They're saying its unusually chilly here for February.'

'I don't get out much. I'm retired, unlike you who is still slogging away.'

I said, 'Retirement doesn't mean stopping work. You can do something else, what you are passionate about. Like Don. You know he took early retirement from Frozen Air six months after the incident with Rana at the plant.'

'I heard. How come the MD let him go?'

'Well he went on to a larger playing field. And helped Frozen Air quite a bit from his new position. He joined politics, you see. In fact, the Congress party wooed him out of the corporate world by giving him a legislative assembly election ticket in a bid to cash in on his popularity in the region. The rest, as they say, was chemistry. The people loved him; he was their hero who'd freed them from Rana's reign of terror. Don won by a thumping margin and, owing to his background, immediately was catapulted to the post of Minister of Industries in a coalition government between the Congress and the Samajwadi Party. After this I didn't keep track of Don's further exploits as I got caught up in interventions initiated as a part of The Collective.'

'Please let's not start with your damn lies. It's really depressing to hear your pathetic fantasies about this fictitious Collective of yours.' Loquacious took a sip from his glass of wine.

I was glad to see some of the old aggression coming back. 'All right, anyway, here we are. What's your wifi password? Let's search for Don...'

From the web links that appeared on my laptop screen, we pieced together the rest of Don's story. There were many links which took us to official sites of the state government which we didn't bother to open. Some newspaper reports told us that as Minister for Industries Don's popularity in the state had soared with a slew of decisions he'd taken using a participative process he called the Ownership Barometer. At the core of it was an Internet and SMS poll his ministry conducted every month on major policy decisions.

A recent interview with a national news channel showed he looked exactly the same. In the conversation, among other things Don told the interviewer that after two terms at the state level he had his eyes on the centre and was aiming for a parliamentary ticket in the next general election. He was all set to be the oldest debutant in the Lok Sabha. I hadn't bothered to follow the election; imagine if the knight of La Mancha had made it to that collective – the mecca of Good Samaritanism. He could be a valuable ally in fulfilling The Collective's agenda.

The last link on the list opened a popular matrimonial site, which had this advert, almost five years old, under Don's name:

> TALL IN STATURE, HANDSOME IN DEEDS, YOUNG IN MIND, MATURE IN YEARS, SOLID IN EXPERIENCE, VIRGIN AT HEART.
>
> IS LOOKING FOR A BIG-BUILT NATURAL BEAUTY WHO SHOULD BE WILLING TO SHARE HER GROOM WITH THE ENTIRE NATION.

Thankfully, there was no photograph of the prospective groom. I wondered how many responses this advert had attracted.

We had a good laugh and decided to go out and buy another bottle of Californian wine. On the way back from the supermarket, a light snow had begun to fall. As we parked the car near his apartment block, I suggested we look up the life histories of Godfather and Rana.

'Also Rocinante! Let's find out what happened to her...' Loquacious whispered as he opened the door with his key. I suppose he was whispering because we were smuggling the bottle of wine into the sanatorium and he didn't want his neighbour to know.

We went back to the deck and sat under the awning. The snow and the sequoias somehow felt like the idle backdrop to our travel down memory lane. Godfather, it turned out, had taken sanyas after the betrayal. He popped up in our search as the chief administrator of an Osho ashram up in the lower Himalayas near Ranikhet. Now that I thought about it, he had been handed a pretty raw deal; after all he'd done for the family and the firm, the way his ouster had been manipulated was quite shameful; I won't ever get a lump in my throat on account of the ogre but that evening in California I joined Loquacious in condemning the treatment meted out to him. After all, he'd meant well for Frozen Air though he might have been somewhat heavy-handed in his ruling style.

Before Loquacious could jump into a well of misery, I tried to change the mood by googling Rana Vidroh Bahadur Singh. The search threw up the same matches I had found earlier, before our meeting with him at the farmhouse. I clicked on a few that refreshed our memories of the man's exploits prior to our encounter with him but there was no link hinting about what had transpired in his life following the Frozen Air fiasco. Presumably he had been sidelined by Don's ascent in the political firmament of the region.

Rocinante's name threw up no links whatsoever and we were settling back disappointedly to our glasses of wine when Loquacious asked me to type 'Janice Kramer' into the search engine.

The links that came up for her name, not surprisingly, showed how influential she was on Wall Street; the slant in her portfolio towards investments in India and China had given her a name as a sort of expert in the South Asian region and she was often quoted in articles or interviewed on television for her views on these growing economies. She had resigned as the head of Mcsinki soon after the Unified Air and Frozen Air deals, concentrating on her portfolio and her family. It was when I clicked on a hyperlink underlining the latter that I fell off my chair.

A photograph of her fourth husband, his hands linked with hers in a cosy pose, stared at us from the middle of the page. I gulped and looked again; the moustache was gone, making it hard to recognize Rana, but the fierce look in his eyes was unmistakable. The caption below said: 'Janice and her current husband, a scion from the state of Uttar Pradesh in India, live together in a sprawling mansion close to Yosemite National Park, California.'

I looked at Loquacious, who was smiling mischievously; I asked him, 'Did you know about this?'

'Ya, you think only you can have secrets. Their mansion is bang opposite this building. When I take my evening stroll, I've seen them leaving together in their limousine on a couple of occasions. You can close your mouth now, Sancho. Got you, didn't I?'

On occasions like this it would feel like Loquacious's condition was improving, until the conversation invariably drifted to Pause's 'hard-heartedness' in rejecting his proposal in the aftermath of the victory against Rana.

'Why are you doing that, Loquacious?'

'What?'

'Clenching and unclenching your fist.'

'I didn't even realize I was doing it.'

'Maybe you shouldn't drink any more.'

'C'mon, Sancho, give my glass back. Don't treat me like a kid. Let me fantasize a bit. Suppose… just suppose, she had accepted my proposal. She was in love with me, you know.'

'Uh,' I grunted in reply. 'Stop clenching your fist, Loquacious, you'll break the glass. Man, you are nervy. Do you need to take some medication or something?'

Usually, I would try to steer the conversation into more cheerful topics; except his desire to wallow in the piteous illusion of his phantom love affair was so staunch he would drag me into the fantasy as well. Sometimes when I saw his condition was bad, I would play along and fib through my teeth to him. But that night the lies got to me. There's no justification for my actions but hearing the sounds of the sequoia grove and watching their giant silhouettes that had stood here for thousands of such twilights must have had something to do with me blurting out the truth that evening. Of course, the wine too played its part in my rashness.

I remember the question that started me off. 'Do you know where she is now?' The illness had made him lose a lot of weight and he was almost as skinny as me by then. He'd never directly asked me about her whereabouts before.

I don't know what came over me; I think it was the pathetic hope in his face. I came clean. 'We live together now.' I have to admit I felt light after this admission.

What he felt was obvious from his reaction. His gaunt cheeks, which had been suffused with the redness from the wine, suddenly lost their colour; from the tremor in his flared nostrils, you could see he was fighting to keep his tears at bay and the knuckles on his clenched fists were almost as white as the snow.

His voice breaking, he said, 'Deep down... I knew.' Had he ever admitted to being in the dark, the poor sod? 'But why did you keep the secret from me all these years? Why didn't you tell me, you bastard? ' He said it quietly, but you could see he was brimming with hurt and rage. 'Are you two married?'

I nodded sheepishly. I shouldn't have been feeling guilty but I was. We had decided to keep the news from him for his own good. Still.

'When?' he barked. His eyes were still shut.

'Remember that evening before we left for Rana's farmhouse, I told you we were late because I was losing my virginity. To her.'

'Oh God!' He covered his ears. 'How crass! Way back then? During the prime of our friendship, you were cheating on me?'

I was drunk now with the headiness of at last blurting out the truth to him. 'We weren't cheating you, Loquacious. You were cheating yourself. You had nothing going with Pause. It was all in your head. She was a mother to you but could never be your wife...' I waited for him to respond; he didn't say anything, he seemed overwhelmed. I continued; I had to absolve myself of the guilt somehow. 'And I didn't seduce her away from you. She initiated the intimacy thing.'

We sat silently for a long time in the gathering gloom, watching the freak snowfall drop on the massive branches of the sequoias. The snow slid off the branches almost immediately, as if eternity was shaking off the moment with a shrug; the moment didn't really have a chance did it? Suddenly I felt inconsequential in front of the trees. What was my puny life in comparison to theirs?

'Does she ever ask about me?' Loquacious broke the oppressive hush.

'No. We've decided not to talk about you. She felt it was best that way. She loved you but not in the way you loved her...'

I broke off for I could tell he wasn't listening anymore. The least I could do was spare him the lip. His eyes were on a large snowflake freshly fallen on the floor of the balcony. As it melted slowly, Loquacious clenched his fist around the wine glass. When it broke none of us reacted; wine mingled with blood flowed in rivulets down his forearm towards his elbow imitating a network of veins. He kept staring at the snowflake long after it was gone. 'I'm lost. I want to go home,' he said softly.

'Me too. I have to prepare for tomorrow's lecture.'

'Lecture? I thought you had come to UCLA to study?'

'No I have been teaching Organizational Development to Master's students at the Xavier Labour Relations Institute for almost five years.'

'XLRI Jamshedpur? That's a premier institute.'

'Yes. And UCLA called me to teach a paper on Ownership for the final year of their Master's Programme on Learning Organizations. After I finish, in the summer I'm off on a lecture tour at eight Ivy League colleges on the same topic.'

'But you don't have a fancy degree if I remember? And no PhD at all…'

I didn't tell him I had no degree at all. Neither did I tell him to close his mouth. 'Experience teaches you more than words ever can,' I repeated to him; something I never tired of telling my students. 'Pause and I have initiated many experiments through The Collective on Ownership and the results have been startling. In any case the only university worth going to is the university of life. Imagine if the world were our classroom…'

Acknowledgments

This book is an outcome of the freedom to experiment with my life, given to me by my parents, my colleagues at Vyaktitva and Pravah, and by the circumstances I was lucky to be born into.

Another stroke of luck was stumbling upon the editorial team of Nandita Aggarwal and Shivmeet Deol at Hachette who played an excellent good cop-bad cop routine and were instrumental in my cutting this experiment to size.

In the final stages, Yunus Patel saved the experiment from a near-fatal blow by warding off a deadly word flu virus attack.

The Boss is NOT Your Friend

Vijay Nair

A handbook for Indian managers to survive all things organizational

Appalled by the latest Radia revelations about your corporate heroes?

Sick of the 'nurturing talent like tiny plants' spiel doled out by most management manuals?

Wondering why they never acknowledge the ugly truth about success: that the trick is either to use your cunning and flattery to rise to the ranks of those who lay down the rules, or at least learn how to massage the egos of the rule makers?

Here finally is a candid, hands-on guide to surviving in the Indian corporate world, complete with a questionnaire to help you identify the particular malevolent subspecies your boss can be classified under.

Designed as a handbook for the Indian executive to survive and prosper, the wisdom it contains is pertinent – if not very nice.

'With its immensely witty, crackling prose, *The Boss is Not Your Friend* reads almost like a black comedy.' Unbound Writers

'Did you think your boss was your pal? Think again, or better still, read Vijay Nair's book, *The Boss is Not Your Friend*. Besides being funny, it provides a rare insight into every conceivable variety of boss.' – *India Today*

For further details and information please visit www.hachetteindia.com

Bangalore Calling

BRINDA S. NARAYAN

Fifteen linked stories set in a call centre in Bangalore

The employees at the Callus call centre in Bangalore juggle false identities, abusive customers and the tugs of family and community.

An Anglo-Indian trainer is aghast at the overt Americanisms adopted by her eager trainees. A van driver who yearns for a son petitions the god Ayyappan by playing devotional songs inside the van. A brash, Jimi Hendrix-loving agent tries to change the music and stokes the driver's deep resentment. A young girl travels across the great divide between the slum she lives in and the shiny glass complex where she works as a toilet cleaner.

Through fifteen linked stories, *Bangalore Calling* explores the social costs of outsourcing — the erosion of cultures, the displacement of vernacular languages and accents — in a world that's not yet flat.

'In this lively and deeply telling collection, the author transports us into an Alice in Wonderland Bangalore call centre training session in which students learn broad–"a" American English, imagine American cities and don take-home American names. They create an offshore piece of America. *Bangalore Calling* is more than a book; it is a powerful wake-up call to look sharp at the cultural core of global capitalism.' – Arlie Hochschild, author of *The Managed Heart: The Commercialization of Human Feeling*

'Entertaining and humane, *Bangalore Calling* is very much a book of our times. It is both a moving introduction to the strange world of the Bangalore call centre, and a reminder of the human and cultural costs of globalization.' – Sam Miller, author of *Delhi: Adventures in a Megacity* and former BBC correspondent in India

**For further details and information please visit
www.hachetteindia.com**

Hachette India is the Indian arm of Hachette UK, the largest and one of the most diversified trade book publishers in the United Kingdom. The other Hachette Group Company imprints include:

Hodder and Stoughton: • Hodder • Sceptre • Hodder Faith • Mobius

John Murray

Headline Book Publishing: • Headline • Headline Review • Business Plus UK • Springboard • Little Black Dress

The Orion Publishing Group: • Orion Books (including Asterix) • Weidenfeld & Nicolson • Phoenix Paperbacks • Cassell • Orion Paperbacks • Orion Children's Books • Gollancz • Everyman Classics

Little, Brown Book Group UK: • Little, Brown • Abacus • Virago • Orbit • Atom • Sphere • Hachette Audio • Piatkus

Hachette Book Group USA: • Center Street • Faith Words • Grand Central Publishing • 5 Spot • Aspect • Business Plus US • Forever • Mysterious Press • Springboard Press • Twelve • Vision • Walk Worthy Press • Wellness Central • Little, Brown US • Ansel Adams • Back Bay Books • Bulfinch • Little, Brown Books for Young Readers • LB Kids • Megan Tingley Books (MT) Books • Poppy • Orbit • Yen Press

Octopus Group: • Hamlyn • Cassell Illustrated • Conran • Philips • Bounty • Gaia • Spruce • Godsfield Press • Mitchell Beazley

Hachette Children's Books: • Enid Blyton • Rainbow Magic • Orchard • Wayland • Franklin Watts • Hodder Children's Books

Chambers-Harrap: • Chambers Dictionaries • Larousse

Hodder Education: • Teach Yourself • Arnold • Philip Allan Updates • Bailey & Love • Michel Thomas Method

With companies in France, Spain, Australia, New Zealand